WRING
A ROAD KILL MC NOVEL
VOLUME 5

New York Times Bestselling author
MARATA EROS

http://marataeroseroticaauthor.blogspot.com/

Marata Eros FB Fan Page: https://www.facebook.com/pages/
Marata-Eros/336334243087970

*Cover art by **Willsin Rowe***

*Editing suggestions provided by **Red Adept Editing.***

ISBN-10: 1979565902
ISBN-13: 9781979565905

WORKS BY TAMARA ROSE BLODGETT

The **BLOOD** Series
The **DEATH** Series
Shifter **ALPHA CLAIM**
The **REFLECTION** Series
The **SAVAGE** Series
Vampire **ALPHA CLAIM**
&
Marata Eros
A Terrible Love (***New York Times*** Best Seller)
A Brutal Tenderness
The Darkest Joy
Club Alpha
The **DARA NICHOLS** Series
The **DEMON** Series
The **DRUID** Series
Road Kill MC Serial
Shifter **ALPHA CLAIM**
The **SIREN** Series
The **TOKEN** Serial
Vampire **ALPHA CLAIM**
The **ZOE SCOTT** Series

DEDICATION
Camilla Olina T.

The spoken and written word—any talent, finesse or success that I possess—I owe to you. I loved you, Mom. I love you still.

I am forever…your Darling.

MUSIC THAT INSPIRED ME DURING THE WRITING OF WRING

Skin

by Beth Hart

1

WRING

I bolt upright in my bed, the upper half of my body dripping sweat. My eyes automatically scan the room. Finding nothing but shadows seeking me from half-closed drapes, I toss myself backward against the soft pillows of my bed, trying to calm my racing heart.

Easier fucking said than done.

Flinging a forearm over my eyes, I force myself to take in my surroundings, moderating my breathing with a familiar, deliberate rhythm.

I'm not in the sandbox.

I'm staying in the fucking boondocks of Ravensdale. Having a place built in rural Orting. The club's letting me stay here until my house is finished.

After a full minute of coming to myself, I sit up, swinging my legs over the side of the narrow bed. My feet find purchase on the lukewarm scarred wood floor of the cabin.

Running a hand over my flat top buzz cut, I let a final shaky breath escape. My heart is still coming down from the nightmare adrenaline buzz.

Probably not one hundred eighty beats a minute. Maybe just one sixty now. Fucking Afghanistan. Got an honorable discharge. I'm tough as fuck…except for the dreams.

The nightmares won't let me go. I've done my time, and now, my commitment runs to less patriotic endeavors.

Like Road Kill MC.

I wish my brain could switch gears. Consciously, I've made the commitment, and my years of service, violence, and chaos are behind me. Subconsciously, the brain won't release me from my obligations. As a knotter. As a SEAL.

I rub circles on my chest, trying to ease the panic that seizes me like one of the knots I so skillfully execute.

Slower. Heart stops galloping. Fucking finally.

I take more deep breaths, letting them out in measured increments. Fucking shrink told me to own my physical body and the rest might follow.

Not working.

Naked, I stand and pad across the confining space of the cabin to the fridge and open it. It's a fucking antique, groaning and burping its displeasure all day long.

All night long.

A couple of lonesome beers stand crooked in the drawer, along with a bunch of science experiment shit.

I chuckle. *Nice.*

I grab a beer and take off the metal top with my college ring. Naval Academy. I take a lot of flak from the brothers for being a college graduate. Whatever. Dad was a graduate. Seemed like if I could follow in those footsteps, I should.

When Dad died from a heart attack, I turned SEAL.

Or the Navy turned me SEAL.

My lips twitch. Yeah, they pretty much turned me. I was a mess. And the boys saved my ass.

They're my family now—Noose, Lariat, and even dumbass Snare, who's really *not* dumb. Fun to razz his ass, though.

I roll the chilled bottle across my forehead, still feeling kind of spooked from the memories that claw their way up my throat in screams I don't voice.

I take a long pull, set the bottle down on the narrow countertop beside the fridge, and walk to each of the windows and the door.

Securing the perimeter.

Natural as breathing. Not having any fucker sneak up on me.

My exhale is frustrated. Should have taken Noose or Snare up on their offer of a room instead of this bumfucked Egypt location that is so soundless, it seems like I'm the only person in the world.

I shake my head, denying the thought as soon as it intrudes. Yeah, that'd been great. Yelling my guts out in the middle of the night while their kids are trying to sleep? *Don't think so.*

I can just hear the questions now. *"Daddy, why does Uncle Wring freak out in the middle of the night?"* That would be the one from six-year-old Charlie, and Aria, Noose and Rose's new kid, isn't even sleeping through the night half the time.

Don't want to fuck up other people's lives. Don't want to see pity in Rose's eyes and empathy in Noose's.

Ditto at Snare's. *Now that he knocked his sister up again.* I chuckle. It is abso-fucking-lutely choice to work Snare over with the sister angle. Does't matter that fuck of a father, Riker, is gone from this earth. Technically, they're not even step siblings anymore. Still entertaining to yank his chain.

I scrub my scalp, feeling the prickle of my short blond hair. The pale color was a hassle when we were stealth. Had to be blacked out. I'm fucking white bread and hate not blending in. My looks didn't help the fun torture I went through, playing with the locals in Afghanistan.

Nope. They weren't partial to my all-American good looks. I didn't fucking care. And that attitude is a bad combination during interrogation.

Read: torture.

Probably not as hard as Noose—Sean King is some kind of other species of crazy—but I'm damn close. We watched each other's backs. Sometimes that camaraderie hurt the three of us, but mostly, it felt damn solid.

I press my forearm against the wood divider that separates the panes of glass inside the antique cabin window. The glass is cold as the day turns gray, night breathing its last breath.

As I watch, bright white light washes the sky, singeing the tops of the trees to low-burning torches. When the red of daybreak creeps over the top of the woods, light like scarlet blood sears everything in its path.

Too bad that fire can't cleanse my ass of the past.

I take another pull of my beer, watching my millionth dawn claim the day, thinking I barely have the fucking sack to see another.

The Harley Davidson Fat Boy feels almost as good as a sweet butt between my legs.

Low purring vibrates in all the right places, but doesn't talk back.

I smirk.

My smile fades as I think about Noose and Snare and what they have. A woman who backs them.

Who they can sleep with.

I crave that intimacy almost more than fucking. I've sexed every club whore in Road Kill—I'm not short on tail.

What I really want is to wake up next to a woman. To feel the silk and warmth of her soft curvy body next to my hard one.

I squeeze my eyes against the image. No bitch who can take what the night brings me.

The nightmares steal the hope of anything permanent. So I just fuck. Eat. Shit. Exercise. Sleep. Repeat.

It's a life, just not the one I wanted. Not the one I planned for.

If it weren't for Road Kill, I wouldn't be here. I slip the kickstand up and roll out of the rural driveway, giving a last look at the small homestead that Viper inherited from his great-grandparents. *Morhorse*? Something like that. It's not Vipe's last name, but I guess the family was a big deal back in the day. Homesteaded Kent, had a few holdings in Ravensdale.

Viper's place is tucked between two copses of trees, a small log gem, gleaming like a piece of fossilized amber.

Viper gets after the place, comes up here for the solitude, likes restoring shit on his spare time.

I turn away. The low rumble of my modified pipes thunder as I cruise slowly down a winding dirt road that's half a mile long. I cram a cig in my craw, willfully abusing my health, and take a deep drag. I sit at the end of the drive, blowing out smoke as the deep colors of dawn wash the clouds tangerine. A long ribbon of emerald-green grass bisects the middle of the gravel drive.

Prospects come out here and mow the swath of grass once a week—in between cleaning up after the club parties. Been six years since I patched in. Didn't take long for Lariat, Noose, and me to get through the fucked-up prospect slavery period.

Guess we just fit in faster. My smile is small, but the memories of being a fucking prospect are still fresh.

We like passing on the baton. I think of Trainer—his dumbass finally patched in. So young he can barely grow a beard.

I got one. It's square and almost white it's so blond. I have one of those tiny clear elastic bands keeping it Fu-Man-Chu style and out of my face when I'm eating road.

Like now. My bike growls as I pull away, leaving Vipe's cabin behind.

Not much traffic as I take 516 all the way through Covington. Used to be Kent-Kangley. Maybe it still is. Kent's such a piece of shit now. I guess it's better than Federal Way, where Noose is from. Auburn, the town between the two, is an armpit too, from what Lariat says of his old stomping grounds.

But we're Southend boys—the club—all of us. And the illegals and gangs aren't pushing us MC men out even though they want to take over our territory.

Road Kill MC rides. We own the road and ourselves. We make our own rules. This is fucking America. Not a cesspool for those fucks to run over the top of citizens and innocents just trying to make a couple of bucks to keep their shitty hamster wheel spinning.

We run the shit we feel like pushing. We don't hurt chicks. We stay relatively clean, keeping to the guns and the occasional drug theft from the gangs.

That's always fun. The first real grin of the day breaks across my face.

Getting closer to the clubhouse, I hit 132nd and head north. Then east again on 224th. When I get to the 196th turnoff, I quickly survey the area. Not seeing shit for movement.

Of course, it *is* seven o'clock in the fucking morning on Sunday.

I'm probably the only swinging dick stirring in the MC cauldron.

I chuckle as I pull up to the club. The gravel parking lot is filled with bikes from last night's kegger, and I can faintly make out the faraway white noise of Highway 18. We're on the back side, sandwiched by Fairway to the north, Kent to the south, and Maple Valley to the southeast.

Good location. After the bullshit with Chaos Riders and the big cop/fed sting a few months back, Viper thought it was a smart idea to come up with a new location on the down low.

So the proposed pole barn became an exhaustive and expensive old building haul instead. Got the old structure at auction. Just had to pay a local outfit to move it to the property the Prez already owned.

Simple.

Except it wasn't. Kent has a bunch of lame fucking environmental laws that needed addressing. Impact fees up the ass. A real pain in the ass to own dick around here now.

Got lucky, though, and found a sympathizer to the club within the ranks of the zealotry of county planners and bullshittery. He greased the wheels for Road Kill.

No, we didn't have any bald eagles, spotted fucking owls, or marshland to save. Just set the building on a concrete foundation and be done with it.

I kill the engine on my custom candy-red painted Harley-Davidson Fat Boy then listen to the engine ticking as it cools. The birds and wind in the trees join the faint music of the highway.

My eyes travel to the clubhouse again. Noose and Lariat worked their asses off getting the interior into shape. Noose is a mechanic, but his skill set extends to carpentry, and Lariat's dad was a plumber.

They took a World War II artillery bunker and made it into a work of art. Bedrooms and shared bathrooms take up the second floor. The girls had bitched and whined until the guys relented and put a glass-topped garden thing on the top. The prospects clean that too.

My lips twist.

Finally got smart and did the lower floor with an all-poured concrete finish. Easier for the prospects to mop up the cum and booze fests. I grin. The other place we'd been leasing before this outfit had to go. Too many rules, building too beaten to fuck to save.

I shield my eyes as chiseled light pierces the dense canopy of western red cedar trees with drooping branches that flank the corners of the structure. At the front and back, trees have been thinned to allow light in so the girls can cultivate plants and shit at the top.

I shake my head. Can't imagine being that whipped. But Noose and Snare are different men since they got women.

Not worse men. Harder. Fiercer. They got something worth protecting, and they're more than who they were, not less.

Bright light nails the paint job of my bike, turning it to gleaming scattered rubies.

I stand, sloughing off my jacket, and stuff it inside my saddlebag. My cut moves like a second skin, creaking as I unlock my trunk, bend, and hassle with reorganizing my shit.

Just as I straighten, the front door to the club sweeps open, and Noose struts out, lighting up as he approaches me. Usually, I'm not blown away by his size. But as the shadows release him from the border of the building, sunlight strikes him like branded fire, and he looks like a giant waking up from a nap.

Tools whack his legs from the belt riding his hip as he saunters toward me. Noose stops in his tracks, hiking his chin. "What ya looking at?" He shoots smoke rings at the sky.

I lift a shoulder. "You're a big fucker." Images of him using his size during our time together in the Middle East slides through my mind like smoke.

Noose's lips tweak at the edges. "Yeah."

I give an abrupt laugh.

"Just noticed?" Noose's eyebrow rises.

I shake my head.

He frowns, switching gears. Reading me like a fucking book. "Not sleeping?"

Don't want to chat about that shit. I blow out an exhale, not bothering to hide my irritation.

Noose studies my locked-up expression. "Hey, man, whatever—Aria's keeping me and Rose up. Feel like a fucking zombie." He cranks his free arm up behind his head, rasping a hand over his longish hair and making it go a million directions. He flicks his cig on the gravel and stomps it out, ripping his hair back and tying it at his nape with one of those hair tie things.

Makes his face look naked—and hard—without the hair.

I fold my arms, kicking my chin up. "So you come here at the ass crack of dawn to do work? That's restful."

Noose nods, cupping his hand around his lighter. The glow from a fresh cig flares in the diffused light.

"When's this mess getting paved?" I kick a loose pebble and it skitters, landing close to Noose's black boot.

Noose's lip rises, baring his teeth. "Not fucking soon enough. Hate gravel with the ride." His palm sweeps out at his machine glinting in the sunlight like a black pearl. A faint layer of dust covers all that chrome and black.

I nod. Yeah—a filthy ride blows.

"How much longer?" I ask, my gaze on the all-concrete building. Windows like the many eyes of an insect ride the top perimeter, looking down on us with glass scorn.

Gloomy fucking thing. As much as I hate to admit it, maybe a garden at the top won't be too bad.

"Impenetrable as fuck," Noose says, easily plucking my thoughts out of thin air.

"Yeah," I answer softly. He's right. Looks like a square hunk of concrete from the outside, but it's the Rock of Gibraltar. Fortification is the goal. Keeps brothers and bitches safe. Snare probably loves the thing.

"A couple of weeks, give or take," he answers, waffling a palm back and forth as he lights his third cig. "Lariat's having some bullshit problems with proper pipe fall for the head."

My lips tweak at the military term for *bathroom*. Noose isn't much for change.

"It's just county code bullshit. Gotta have a certain percentage of fall so all the growlers and shit can go where they gotta go. Can't have turds getting lost." He shrugs, but his lips curl into a faint smile. Nothing like referencing toilet habits for comedic relief.

We laugh.

"So you still up at the cabin?"

Noose's eyes meet mine.

"Yeah." I look away. "Quiet up there. House is about done."

We stand in comfortable silence while he smokes. Neither of us has to talk.

Soon, I join him.

"Kinda boondock shit you got happening out by Snare. Love living in the city," he admits.

"Yeah, lot of noise there." I don't say how backfire from cars makes me think of enemy gunfire.

Noose already knows.

I guess we all react differently to war. Quiet gives me some peace. Noise is disorienting as fuck. Panic loads my shorts like shit.

Don't fucking need that.

"Who'd you say was building your pad?"

"Custom home outfit. Terhune."

"Ah." Noose tilts his head, brows meeting. "Yeah. Remember that now. Seen their building down in the valley."

More silence.

"It's better now with Rose."

My heart picks up stray beats. "What?" Can't help the hoarseness in my voice—the warning.

Noose looks at me. "The nightmares and shit. The sweats, the fucking shakes."

I blink. "You—what the fuck is this?" I pop my jaw back. "Confession time?"

Noose shrugs his broad shoulders. "Trying to help."

"Don't." My eyes narrow.

"All right, having a woman you care about—sounds stupid." Noose looks down, shaking his head. He flicks an ash half a finger long. It falls like gray rain beside his shit kicker.

I wait. Finally, when he doesn't talk anymore I say, "All right—fuck it. What?"

He looks up. "We're killers, Wring. You, me, Lariat— hell even Snare has come around." A smile ghosts his lips. "But"—he looks up at the sky, lighting his fourth cigarette in forty minutes—"Rose makes me feel safe." His voice is a thread between us.

I snort. "No fucking way. You could kill five people with your eyes closed. Our hands, our weapons—*we're* lethal. How does a slip of a woman without skills make *you* feel safe, Noose?"

His neck reddens. "Not here." He taps his temple. "Here, man." Noose's hand moves to his heart.

Our eyes lock, and suddenly, the silence is awkward. His words cling to me.

Suffocating me.

I turn around on my booted heel and march my ass back to the ride.

Noose follows, his heavy treads matching mine.

He grabs my arm, and I spin around. Angry, frustrated, and more exhausted than I have a right to be.

"Don't," I say in a low voice.

"I don't fucking dream anymore."

I rip my arm from his grasp. "Good for *you*."

Noose flings his arms away. "'Kay, you stubborn fuck. I'm done with sharing the feels with your tenacious ass."

"Good," I say, hopping on my bike. I can't take his brand of encouragement. Can't accept it. *Why doesn't he leave well enough the fuck alone?*

Noose doesn't say anything.

I blast away, kicking up a spray of gravel on the temporary gravel driveway.

I run, using my bike to carve distance.

Noose's words chase me.

2

SHANNON

I smooth my long thick hair back into a low knot at my neck.

Getting ready for story time at the Kent Public Library has me wanting to look the part. My eyes rove my form in the silvered antique full-length mirror set diagonally in the corner of my tiny room.

A slim-fitting but proper-length pencil skirt grazes just above my knees. I've paired the conservative navy skirt with a shell blouse in ivory without a hint of yellow. It shows no cleavage but still outlines my figure perfectly. Two-inch heels offer enough style to keep me out of "meh" territory. It's the only place to work within walking distance, so I don't need a car.

There's no money for that.

As it is, our little house is flanked by two commercial warehouses in the Kent Valley. At only one thousand square feet and pre–1940 construction, the anomalous little house is seated in prime real estate. It's a holdover from an era when a bunch of houses just like ours dotted the Kent Valley—mainly homesteads for local farms that had since been eaten up my technology and commerce. Our tiny place had once belonged to my great-grandfather. It'd actually served as a cottage, an outcropping of a larger farmhouse, long gone now.

Our cottage survives on a sixteenth of an acre out of the original forty. Mom owns that small sliver, the remaining property is gone. The property taxes are so high, I barely have enough to keep us in food. Because Mom's health is so dire, I can only hold a part-time job. Someone needs to take care of her.

My pensive face stares back at me, life's troubles tumbling around inside my head like clothes in a dryer.

A cup shatters, and my shoulder's slump from their regularly erect posture. *Why does she try?* Breathing through my irritation, I try to calm my nerves and smooth my skirt with damp palms.

Mom needs me.

I pivot then stomp out of my room. I'm completely prepared to chastise—until I see her stooped over the shattered tea cup. Her soft tears splash on the worn linoleum, cracked and abused from its long life, as her grief sinks into the floor's decaying crevices.

"I'm sorry, Shannon. I just, I know how hard you're working. I want to *do* something. To matter."

My heart breaks, and I rush over there, helping Mom up. Careful to avoid her hands, I extend my forearm, and she places the flat of her palms on my arm. She pushes off at the same time as I lift, and we get her on her feet.

What if she'd fallen instead of just trying to bend over to clean up the shards?

"Mom," I say gently, "you can't do stuff like this before your meds have kicked in."

The meds that are killing her.

She nods quickly, her steel-colored, chin-length hair flowing forward in a curtain.

I guide Mom slowly to her favorite chair and arrange the pillows to cushion her fragile and inflamed joints.

The rheumatoid arthritis has robbed her of agility, strength, and most importantly—her freedom.

The medication she's taken since I was eighteen months old has weakened her muscle tissue.

Including the heart.

Take *this* medication or never move. Take it and eventually have a heart attack.

Great options.

So Mom took the medication so she could care for her child and herself. When the disease progressed enough to cripple her body, she still took it.

Then I stayed with her instead of pursuing anything for myself.

There are no benefits for someone who's never worked and gets struck down by a disease during youth. So Mom had me at thirty-seven. And now she's only sixty-two.

Medicare doesn't kick in until age sixty-five.

She won't live to see it, though. The doctors have made that much clear. And we might not hang on to this house until then.

I can't allow that to happen.

I can't let anyone take this house before Mom dies.

Not the tax authorities for delinquent payment. Not the gang members who have moved into both the commercial buildings and sandwich our property like rotting meat.

I shiver.

But how's one twenty-five-year-old, part-time librarian supposed to fight the money men—or the gangs?

"You look nice, Shannon," Mom says through a watery smile, breaking into my thoughts.

My constant worries slide away at the expression on her face. Anxiety, regret, and guilt. "Thanks, Mom."

Though her hair is solid pewter now, and her wrinkles are few. The ones that mark her face are in the right spot. By her eyes.

Proof of all the smiles.

Pale blue eyes blink up at me, and I do a quick scan of the immediate area. Water jug with large handles and integral straw. Check. Meds laid out. Check.

Lunch pail. Check.

She has the remote to the TV—but even better than that is the pile of newspapers, magazines, and nonfiction books. Mom adores reading.

I know that's where my love of the written and spoken word came from.

"Go, honey." She smooths her hands down her bony legs, covered by knit sweatpants in an icy lavender color. Her soft cotton broadcloth T-shirt is a matching color. The cotton fabric is all she can stand to wear against her sensitive skin. "I'm fine."

I put my perfect, young hand over her gnarled one. The joints of her fingers are so swollen, they've caused the fingers to cant to one side.

I close my eyes in a long blink, sucking up my emotions into a bottle inside myself. "Okay, Mom."

Tears don't fall. I always cry in my room, where Mom can't see. But I think she knows. Instead of showing my sadness, I gulp back my stupid sniveling and offer a true smile.

"That's my girl." She looks away, gazing out the sparkling clean window at the cars rushing past on the busy street. "You have a good day with the kiddos, honey."

I draw in a fortifying breath. "Don't call me 'honey'—"

"Call me 'darling,'" Mom finishes.

We grin at each other. I've been saying that for years, and she's always replied the same way.

Our private mantra.

I kiss her forehead and move to the door. Solid reinforced steel. I unlatch four locks.

I step through without looking back and relock all of them. I try the knob. Twice.

Five hours away from Mom. *She'll be okay, Shannon.*

I straighten my spine and begin walking the eight blocks to my job. I love it so much. When I was younger, I dreamed of being an elementary school teacher.

Or just maybe filling a home with children of my own. My smile is wistful, and a moment of rare peace passes through me.

It's probably why I don't notice Vincent until his hands are on me.

"Hey cunt," a voice cuts through my musing like a dirty knife.

Then his greasy hands are on me, popping my feet off the sidewalk and pulling me into a small alleyway between the tall commercial buildings.

My eyes slide the three blocks to the faded red dot of the porch overhang on our house. My attention bounces around mournfully—we're very close to Kent Station, but there isn't much traffic this early on a Sunday morning.

No one to help me. "Let go!" I yell at him.

He pinches my upper arm, and I whimper. I keep saying no, hoping the gangs find an easier target.

Not some girl with an invalid mother to take care of.

"Just do what we say, and we'll take care of you, Shannon."

I bite the grunt of pain off mid-sound. "You're hurting me."

"I don't have to," Vincent says oh-so-reasonably. "You spread those pretty legs for me, and I'll see you get *plenty* of work. We have girls that aren't half as good lookin' as you, bitch. You earn the cash on your back—make it easy on your mama." His dark eyebrows hike, and his pinch goes to bruising.

I gasp, and he runs a finger over my lip. I bite the plump flesh to keep from crying out, inciting more violence. "I can get big money for your pussy. Real money." His brows lower over his eyes in an unforgiving line. "Word on the street has it you never been tapped yet."

I feel my eyes go wide as my breathing turns to harsh pants. *They want the house bad enough that they've actually researched me? How would these losers even know that kind of personal information about somebody?*

Calling the cops doesn't help. The fucking gang—an offshoot of the Bloods, I hear—are in possession of police scanners. They scatter like cockroaches, and when the police arrive, they're sympathetic. But without anyone to arrest, it's like I'm reporting a crime where the perpetrators are ghosts.

Hopelessness descends. "I don't have anywhere else to live, for me and my mom to go." I've been trying to reason with them for the last three years, since they moved into the buildings that surround us. But they've begun to push harder.

He nods, a cunning smile spreading over his vile features. "I know, *chica*. Let me put you under my protection. You let me into that house, into your bed—and me and the brothers will take care of your mama and take real good care of you."

He grabs his crotch, and I fight gagging.

Even with an offer as horrible as that, it's so tempting, becoming a whore to this man so I can save Mom. They've been relentless. They push, push, push. And I say no, no, no. Then there's nothing for a time.

I hadn't seen anyone in half a year, and I'd become complacent, hoping they'd found greener pastures. That a couple of defenseless women who didn't have a pot to piss in or a window to throw it out of was just—too much work. I allowed myself to believe that we were finally flying under their radar.

But no.

Here's Vincent. All six feet of threatening dark and deadly to my five feet five of Nordic paleness.

He grabs a strand of hair that's come loose from my bun. "This shit real?" Vincent bends over my hair and sniffs it.

I'm suddenly pissed he wrecked my careful library hairdo. In fact, I'm just flat-out angry in general. Over everything. "What?" I ask in a semi-daze, my upper arm numb from his vise-like grip.

"The fucking hair!" He screams in my face, tearing out the rest of my careful hairstyle. My platinum hair falls almost to my waist, relieved of its binding.

Vincent jerks me against him. "You give me a stiff cock, bitch. All your fucking stuck-up white-girl bitch bullshit. Hiding that hot body underneath your library clothes."

He crowds my neck, scenting me like a stud dog.

I mewl. My rage evaporating to fear so acute, I clench my legs together so I don't urinate four hundred feet from my front door.

"I bet your pussy matches the hair."

A vehicle rumbles past the alley, and Vincent swings his head up in surprise, shoving me up against the building. I slap my palms against the rough brick.

"What the fuck?" he asks in a hoarse voice of interrupted arousal. His hand slides from my hair to my wrist. He pulls me behind him, and I trip, bumping into the back of him. I cry out when my nose rams his shoulder blade.

"Come on, puppy." He gives a harsh tug, and I stumble forward, yelping from the abuse of my wrist.

Gliding toward us is a man, approaching slowly on a really beautiful red motorcycle. The color is like a juicy sparkling apple.

He's as fair as I am. Crisp white-blond hair is shaved close to his head, and a really flat crop of it stands about a half inch on top of his head.

Icy-blue eyes flash at the sight of us standing in the border of the alley, where shadows hide Vincent's violence.

I know the only person that's seen us will roll on by. Just a girl and guy making out in the gloom, he'll assume.

Tears roll down my face, and my wrist is throbbing.

The motorcycle slows. My hope flares. *Please help me,* my eyes beg, despite my heart pulsing sickly in my throat.

Vincent's grip tightens, and new tears follow the old. A hurt gasp escapes between my lips.

"Shut up, snatch," Vincent growls over his shoulder.

Even sitting down on his bike, the man is huge, bigger than the gang creep with his hand on me. His eyes meet mine.

Vincent postures, and he's dangerous. In my mind's eye, he's like a rooster strutting around in the chicken coop.

This man filling my vision doesn't posture. He oozes danger.

His gaze flicks to Vincent.

"Fucking Road Kill mofo," Vincent seethes from between his teeth and spits in the direction of the man. His snotty loogy hits the sidewalk in a gross stream, and I shudder.

The stranger frowns, his bike slowing to a crawl.

Road Kill? I have time to wonder, then he's rolling the great bike to a stop and flipping the kickstand out with the heel of his black boot. The metal tip hits the cement with a final-sounding click.

The bike settles, and the rider sweeps his leg over the seat before hopping to the curb with a grace that has my mouth hanging open.

Up close, his coloring is even more fair than mine. He's like a cool, smooth walking glacier of muscle and menace.

Maybe I shouldn't have begged silently for help. Maybe this is a prime example of jumping from the frying pan into the fire.

His eyes move over me in two seconds, lingering on my face a heartbeat longer, then he turns his attention to Vincent.

Vincent's free hand flexes into a fist. "You got a problem, Road Kill maggot?"

The stranger smiles at Vincent. The expression is so frightening, I take a step back.

I watch Vincent frown at my retreat. Without ever looking at me, he crushes my wrist. I yell helplessly, dropping to my knees.

"Oh God, please." My hand struggles over his to release me.

"Let the girl go."

That voice. It's deep. Articulate. Resonant. The tone strikes me like a wake-up chime, and I ignore the extreme pain, daring to look up.

His crystalline eyes are for Vincent—he never looks at me or acts like I'm even there.

I pant through the grinding white-hot agony of my wrist.

"No, man, she's a whore bitch. Just getting some facts straight between us. Not Road Kill MC biz. You feel?"

Disgust and resignation flash across the stranger's features. Finally, he turns to me, and the full weight of his gaze seizes me, gripping me in a cosmic thrall. I gulp. *Holy hell.*

Who is *he?*

His eyes slim on me with clear disbelief. "This true? You this gang prick's whore?"

Instead of answering, I scream as Vincent mangles my wrist. Stars burst at the sides of my vision, and I sway, beginning to crumple. I hit the sidewalk with my shoulder, and my teeth click together, hard. My wrist is still held in his grip. I can't feel my hand.

"Okay." The stranger steps forward without hesitation and punches Vincent in the nose.

Not a regular, movie type of punch that's all neat and pretty. The hit snaps Vincent's head back like a door got opened in his face.

Releasing my wrist, he folds like a human chair, out cold. His head bounces off the sidewalk, landing with a crack.

I perform a klutzy crab crawl, trying to distance myself from my torturer. I use my hands to push myself up and scream, falling immediately. My wrist is useless.

Strong arms lift me from the cement, and I scream louder. A hand covers my mouth.

"Shut up." His voice fills my ears.

Instantly, I still.

Oh God, oh God, oh God.

"Listen to me, and listen carefully. I'm in the middle of Blood territory, and I need to get the hell out of here. But you answer a question first."

Huh?

He turns me, his hand still covering my mouth. Tears run out of the corners of my eyes; my wrist is a mass of numb heat.

"You going to scream?"

I shake my head. But I'm still scared.

He gently lifts his hand and sets me on my feet.

I fight nausea and the urge to faint. *I will not be weak.*

Vincent groans behind us, and my bladder hiccups.

"You his whore?"

My mouth pops open.

He grins, eyes flicking over my shocked expression. "Didn't think so. Don't have the look." His gaze scrapes down my once-pristine outfit.

Nice. Lech.

I fold my arms, yelp at my wrist.

He frowns. "I can get you somewhere."

Oh. Vincent.

This dangerous man can get me somewhere before Vincent wakes up.

I narrow my eyes, and he waits, looking bored.

"Or you can stay here and take your chances with Mr. Wonderful Gang Leader." He walks closer, towering over me, even though I'm wearing heels. "Unless I misinterpreted the message from those pretty green eyes of yours? You were needing help, right?" he asks in a soft whisper, but somehow, his words are clipped and angry.

I nod, tears scattering before I can stop them.

He scowls, taking my good wrist and hauling me behind him. My heels make a racket, echoing off the concrete. His muscular legs swings over his bike, then he drops my hand and flicks his jaw behind him. "Hop on."

I've never been on a bike before. I don't know him.

Vincent is crawling toward the curb, after us.

"Stay sleeping, fucker, or I'm going to knock your teeth down your throat," the stranger says in casual warning to the crawling Vincent.

"Don't…you…fucking—" Vincent gasps through his ruined nose.

The stranger cups a hand behind his ear. "Don't? You? Fucking?" He slaps his thighs, a dark chuckle shooting out of his mouth like a cannon. "I'm not planning on *fucking* you. Sacks of shit are not on the menu."

"Get on," he barks at me again, and I mimic his mounting of the bike, though I hike up my skirt to mid-thigh to slide on the back. He reaches behind him and cups his hands on my butt, and I gasp as he hitches me against him. "Hang on, blondie."

Blondie?

I slip my hands around his waist, favoring the bad one, and he takes ahold of my uninjured hand. I notice how automatic he is. Smart.

"I got you."

He rolls out of there. The bike shakes between my legs, and his hard body is in front of mine, heating me through his leather vest.

I turn just my head around to look at Vincent, and his angry eyes follow us with death standing in his gaze.

Mom and I will never be safe. This gorgeous stranger just granted us time.

Like a stay of execution.

3

WRING

I feel the vibration in my pocket and with a blatant disregard for the law. I extract my phone from my pocket and glance at the text.

Noose: Don't be a dickbag. Rose is making pancakes.

Fucker. He knows I like Rose's cooking. Especially the pancakes. *Damn.*

I put the cell up to my face and audio my anger into a text.

Me: Keep your nose out of my shit.

A full minute passes.

Noose: I wouldn't do dick if I didn't give a rat's ass.

I know. It's what I need, but I can't accept. Something won't let me.

Noose means well, the stubborn fucker.

I speak my reply, and the letters appear on my phone. I hit Send.

Me: just give it a rest.

Noose: for now. Swing by our place. Have grub.

My eyes watch traffic beginning to finally get on the road on the only lazy day of the week. I tap my fingers. Thinking. Trying not to.

Me: Ok.

I slide the phone back into my inner pocket of my cut and take a right on 240th heading west, toward Noose's.

I cut through Kent Station, a relatively new depot, strip mall and condo complex they threw in the valley a couple of years ago. They did a good job, unlike a lot of older Kent enterprises, where infrastructure and planning were afterthoughts.

I pass a funky old faded red house squeezed between two high-rise commercial buildings on my right, spotting local gang tag shit hidden in plain sight. Symbols are buried in allowed graffiti that looks like artwork. I slow.

Hate this block. The ritzy condo place where Noose lives is only ten blocks from Blood territory. Top Shelf Condos.

It's a tangible distance. Proof of what the Bloods are quietly doing is right here, breathing down our collective necks.

And Road Kill MC is going to make them bleed. We don't allow gangs. All of our charters are working hard to defend territory. It's simple. Basically, if they try to move into ours, we kill them. Sends a permanent message.

Lots of final-looking rope burns decorate gang members throats who thought they would push their agenda. The marks are like a Road Kill MC calling card now.

There's no open casket for those fuckers' funerals.

A loose smile fills my face at the thought of eradicating those shitbags.

My expression and momentary happiness fade at the sight that catches my eye.

Gang leader—don't know his name—sporting Blood colors has a solid hold on a woman.

She's blond, slim, and built to fuck. Not cheap.

I frown. Image doesn't work. Fucking Bloods are starting to sell flesh to get fast cash. This chick doesn't look like a working girl.

Judging by her body language, she's not real *willing*, either.

Next to the tall gang fuck, she looks like a porcelain doll. Long blond hair falls to a shapely ass. Her sexy-secretary getup shows kick-ass acres of smooth fair skin at her arms, legs, and throat. Creamy, not pasty.

I turn away, concentrating on the road and beyond that, Noose's place. He's got food. *Fucking starved.*

My instincts fire off over what I just saw, interrupting my thoughts.

Fuck.

I glance over my shoulder, and green eyes like seawater meet mine. The plea in that gaze turns my stomach.

Don't put your dumb fucking nose in gang shit. No brothers at my back.

You don't know this bitch, Wring. Leave it.

Tears run down her face, as clear as day, sparkling like captured diamonds of sadness.

Fuck it.

I execute a tight U-turn and come around, rolling the bike into the stall. Kill the engine and hop off.

The closer I get, the more I want this fucker to let her go, the feeling creeps over my skin like ants on their favorite hill.

"Fucking Road Kill mofo," the prick says, adjusting his undersized junk.

Hmmm.

He's hurting the woman. I've never been a fan of men putting their hands on females. Find I become less of one all the time.

I stare at this piece of shit, willing him to be smart with my gaze, trying to convince myself to hold back.

"You got a problem, Road Kill maggot?" His jaw kicks up, tempting me with breaking it. My eyes line up on the bulls-eye he's presenting.

That's about the point when I figure I can't hold back.

I smile at him.

The girl is the smartest one of all three of us. She takes a look at my face and steps back.

The fucker clamps down on her wrist, and she falls to her knees, giving a pitiful cry of pain. "Oh God, please."

Adrenaline roars through me, singeing my guts—all of me. I embrace the familiar thrill of it. My body gets loose. Ready. Resigned to the immediate future. "Let the girl go." I'm still giving him a chance.

For me, that's fucking patient.

"No, man, she's a whore bitch. Just getting some facts straight between us. Not Road Kill MC biz. You feel?"

I'm not feeling him. Never will. This girl looks as new as a shiny penny. She doesn't have that weary vibe. Her eyes are pure of the grime of life. I look at her again. *Most of it, anyway.* The type of life this fucker offers hasn't left its stain on her.

I assess that in seconds, but I gotta be sure. "This true? You this gang prick's whore?"

Her mouth opens to answer, and I notice how beautiful she is. Her lips have a deep cupid's bow above the upper lip.

Distracting as fuck.

I lick my lips, committed now.

Then the prick twists her wrist, and she falls against the sidewalk with a yell.

"Okay." I nod decisively, stepping into him like a dance partner.

With my fist.

I strike hard, checking my swing at the last second so I don't actually kill him. An immediate Blood war, we *don't* need.

Man's got to employ a lot of finesse when his hands are considered lethal weapons. I use that now, knocking the idiot out without killing him.

He'll be okay, I muse regretfully.

He drops like a rock, head tapping hard on the sidewalk.

I grin. *Love. It.*

The girl tries to crawl away, and I get a flash of lacy panties and pop a boner right in the middle of the mess.

Well…fuck me.

I snort.

She tries to stand, screams as she puts weight on the arm the gang fuck hurt, and drops, cracking her elbow trying to catch herself.

I stride over there and pluck her off the sidewalk. She's a featherweight. I automatically assess her.

Smells sweet, like ripe peach and yummy female. Maybe a buck fifteen. Five and a half feet tall.

Boner goes full tilt.

She screams and I clamp a hand over her mouth. "Shut up."

The girl stills.

I tell her what's going on. We're knee deep in Blood territory. Where there's one Blood, more will show.

"You his whore?" I ask again, because hurt or not, female or not, that's a different ball of wax.

I don't give her time to answer before firing off another question. My eyes bore into hers, commanding her with my stare to tell me the truth. *Did she want help?*

She nods, sending big crocodile tears flying. I fight a pang of tender for her and want to wipe those big tears off her gorgeous face.

What the hell's wrong with me?

My hands shake as I grab her unhurt arm and haul her behind me, telling her to get on the ride.

Fucker's woken up, and he's crawling toward us.

I smirk.

You think that love tap is all I got? My slight smile becomes a grin. I got *so much* more. Maybe if he sticks around, I'll give him a slice of *hurt ya* pie.

I bark at the girl to get on, calling her Blondie out of nowhere.

She gets on, and her hands tentatively encircle my waist. I grab the uninjured one and put it where it rides more comfortably on my torso.

I'd love to have that small hand on my cock.

My smile stays.

I reach behind me and cup her ass cheeks, hiking her against me. She feels right in my palms.

I roar out of there.

Don't know how I'm going to explain it all when I get to Noose's.

Won't matter.

That brother's got my back. Always has.

I drop the code into the lighted pad with a quick stab of fingers and shoot the girl a look. She stays locked on my bike. My eyes travel her arm, stuttering over the bruising at her delicate wrist.

The underground garage door begins to slide up.

I walk to the bike and get on. Her slender arms come around me again without a word, and I hit the kickstand, rolling underneath the ground.

I park next to Noose's stall. It's empty.

Weird. Feels like that fucked-up little event took forever. I stay seated on the ride, turn the key, and extract my cell to check the time. Straight up ten.

Huh. Not *that* much time.

Blondie says, "I—thank you—I need to get to my job."

I grunt. "Fuck that." Swinging my leg over the seat, I grab her around the waist and set her on her feet. She looks up at me.

Fearful.

Fucking beau-tee-ful. Wow. I've never seen a pair of eyes that green, that deep. I don't know what the fuck, but she wipes all the bullshit swirling around in my tired brain for the moment.

Her bottom lip trembles. "I need this job."

I shake my head. "Too dangerous. That Blood's marked you. He thinks you're his."

Her chin lifts defiantly, and I'm happy to see a glimpse of spirit. "I am *not* his. Vincent doesn't know me. He—" She snaps her mouth shut, crossing her arms, and delicious breasts sort of pop to the top of the shirt she's wearing.

My dick gets hard.

"Vincent, huh?" Rage descends, chasing away my half-erection. She was lying after all, she knows him. Fucking perfect. I grab her shoulders, mindful of her wounded wrist. "He what?"

Her eyes go to fear immediately, and it sucks to see that.

Noose's timing couldn't be better, and he rolls into the slot next to mine. He shuts off his ride and swings around on the seat, takes a look at Blondie and says,

"Who the fuck is this?" he hikes his thumb at her, his eyes moving from the top of her head to the bottom of her scuffed heels.

"None of your business, you hood!" she yells.

Perfect.

Noose stands.

Blondie cowers as his eyes narrow on her. "She some sweet butt?" he asks, inspecting her like an interesting worm.

"Does she look like one?" I ask.

Noose shakes his head slowly. "Nope." A grin starts forming on his smug face.

"I am not—gah! A sweet butt or whatever you're thinking I am." She blushes.

I haven't seen an honest-to-God blush in fucking forever.

Noose starts barking laughter. When he can finally contain himself, I'm scowling. "*This*, I gotta hear." His eyebrow quirks. "The sweet butt who's not—she coming for pancakes?"

"No," she says at the same time I say, "Yes."

We glare at each other. *She doesn't get it.*

My strength of will.

I didn't just step in a pile of shit for nothing. I want to know what I sacrificed the club for. And make no mistake, me taking a woman from a Blood, even one that might not be his, wasn't an amicable move.

It'll be seen as a move in need of retaliation.

"My job—" she begins.

"Fuck that," Noose and I say together.

He grins wider, clearly loving the situation.

We bump knuckles, and I tug her behind me. She comes quietly.

Feels kind of like the calm before the storm to me.

4

SHANNON

I'm getting out of this crazy situation the second I can. But for now, I allow the scary stranger to tow me behind him.

I'm no girl on a leash.

Vincent couldn't figure out how to make me cooperate in the past.

Intimidation hasn't worked. Threats didn't work.

His violence was effective in the moment. But he's a criminal. He would have to kill me to make me comply. I'm not moving my mom out of our house when she's at death's door. Not happening.

I appreciate this guy saving me from Vincent. His methods were similar to Vincent's, but somehow, when they're not used against me, I'm more charitable.

And I really appreciate the view of his hot body. But these two are not going to push me, either. Waiting this out is the only solution for the moment.

We cram into an elevator and begin to rise. Top Shelf condos are for the rich. I've seen this condo complex while walking to the surviving mom-and-pop store not too far from our house. They'll eventually be run out by the Walmarts and the QFCs, just like everything else.

Covertly, I check out the other biker. He's even bigger than the guy who saved me. Not by much, though.

He catches me looking at him, and a brittle smile flashes across stern features.

I shrink back.

"Noose won't hurt ya," my savior says.

Right. I bite back my laughter.

The elevator doors whisper open, and the men step out. I follow hesitantly. There are only two doors on either side of a long corridor laid with rich fabric carpeting in a tiny geometric pattern in jewel tones of violet, scarlet, and emerald.

"Neighbor," Noose says, hiking a thumb at a door. He moves to the other door and raps on the solid wood hard, once.

I hear a little kid racing to the door, footfalls like a herd of elephants. I smile.

"Aunt Rose!"

"Don't open it." Noose says in a menacing low-voiced command.

"Duh," the boy says from the other side of the door.

His smile is tight. "That's right. Good boy, Charlie," Noose mutters with a genuine grin of pride.

I frown. It's all too weird.

Noose leans against the door, fingers spreading across the surface. "It's me, baby."

His hands drop as the door opens, and a woman about my age stands there, with a baby on her hip. Noose pushes his way inside and grabs the young woman, sweeping her and the baby against him.

"Noose!" she laughs.

He kisses her so thoroughly, I look away, cheeks heating.

My savior smirks, rolling his light-blue eyes. "Get a room, pervs."

Noose pulls back. "Fuck off, Wring." He leans in for more, pecking and kissing her.

Wring. I turn to look at him.

"Is that your name?"

He gives me a speculative glance. "Yeah."

I shift my eyes to my shoes.

"Who is she?" the woman asks, giving me a curious once-over.

I focus on the baby girl, while a boy who appears to be about six years old races around.

We recognize each other at the same moment.

"Charlie!" I say in surprise.

"Miss Shannon!"

Wring turns to me, frowning. He appears so tough, so scary. But not when he looks at me. "You know the kid?"

I nod. "He's, ah, he's one of my kids for story time."

"*You're* Miss Shannon?" The woman's smiling now.

"Yes."

"Okay, who the fuck are you, and what's going on?" Noose glowers.

"Noose," the woman says and gets right up beside him, transferring the baby to the other hip. She thwacks him on his big bicep. "Stop being a butt. Can't you see she's freaked out?"

Yeah. *Can't you see it?* I fold my arms, giving out dirty looks to the two men like candy.

"Miss Shannon?" Charlie asks me quietly.

I sink, resting my butt on my heels. I smooth my skirt over my knees and tuck the excess fabric under my rear. I meet eyes that are as brown as the girl's and wrap my arms around my shins. "Uh-huh."

"Why weren't you at story time today?"

Great question. I wonder who filled in.

I wonder if I still have a job. Tears burn the back of my eyes. I rub them viciously. *No* crying.

"Again, who the fu"—the woman belts him again—"are you?"

Wring stares at me, not saying a word.

"I'm sorry. Noose is being *rude*." She sticks out her hand.

I stand, taking it. We shake.

"I'm Rose, and this big lug is my husband, Noose. You've met Charlie, and this beauty is Aria."

The baby's beautiful, like her mom.

The little girl seems to know her name and coos. Then she proceeds to wreck Noose's tough-guy image by grabbing at the end of his hair.

"No, no, princess, don't pull Daddy's hair."

I smile, suppressing a giggle at the Big Bad Biker dude being put in his place by an infant. "I'm Shannon." I look down at my feet again. "I guess you know who I am." I glance up at Rose and include Charlie in the look. My inhale is sharp, regretful. "This gang guy stopped me today and was hassling me—"

"Hurting you," Wring corrects.

I give him a sharp look, nodding at his honest assessment.

I swallow hard, throat suddenly dry in response to the memory of my fear. "He was." Fighting the urge to rub my aching wrist, I quickly look away. It occurs to me that I haven't really used it, favoring that hand.

"Anyway, Wring here…he, uh…he punched him pretty good and—"

"Oh *fuck*." Noose's mouth drops open, and he whips his head in Wring's direction.

Wring grimaces. "Yeah. Couldn't stand it, man."

"Gotcha." Noose shakes his head in disbelief.

I give a helpless shrug. "So here I am, and I missed work today because of him." I can't finish.

"Pancakes?" Rose interjects, and I give her a grateful look.

My mouth waters. I didn't have breakfast. I don't most days. Giving in to hunger is a luxury. Usually, I just wait until supper and have something. Mom's meds tear up the lining of her stomach if she doesn't take them with food.

"You hungry?" Wrings asks into the sudden silence.

"Fuck yes, she is. Looks like a candidate for a food funnel." Noose grins, and Wring frowns.

Rose just shakes her head and begins to walk off. "Follow me, Shannon."

Charlie runs ahead of me, bouncing all the way to the opposite end of the house. "Yay! Pancakes!"

"Lots of energy," Rose comments in a dry voice.

I stifle a smile. "Yes."

Two separate huge pancake stacks are piled sky high on a platter beside heated syrup and a dish of what looks like real butter. A chilled pitcher holds orange juice.

I swallow past the lump of grateful in my throat. "Wow, this is quite a spread."

"Noose doesn't require much," she says with thick sarcasm.

"Food and fucking," Noose replies nonchalantly, and throws an arm around her neck. The baby squeals as Rose blushes furiously.

I'm embarrassed for her, this crude guy. I glare at him.

Then he leans way down, nuzzles her neck, and kisses her temple. "She's fucking great at all that."

He smiles at her like she's the most precious thing in the world, and they touch foreheads.

My embarrassment moves right into envy. Wow, it's so obvious they're in love. He might be crude and rough, but clearly, he adores his family.

Wring takes that moment to lean over the granite countertop on his elbow and pop a grape from a nearby fruit bowl into his mouth. "Pussy whipped," he comments as Noose and Rose have their moment.

I blink. *What have I gotten myself into?*

"You're next," Noose says smugly, pointing a finger at him and pretend shooting.

They exchange a private glance.

"I'm sure Shannon is all worn out after her ordeal and needs food." Rose slips out of Noose's grasp and hands him his daughter. He picks her up and lifts her high into the air. "Better not barf on Daddy," he says, squinting.

Looks like maybe that's happened before. I bite the inside of my lip to keep from laughing.

"Aria probably needs fresh pants." Rose cocks a golden-brown eyebrow high, and he sighs, resigned to diaper duty.

"Man, I used to be cool!" He trudges off to do the deed, and Wring rolls to both elbows on the countertop and props his chin in his hands.

"You were never cool, Noose," he comments in a droll voice.

"Fuck *off!*" he yells from another room.

I smirk. They act like family.

Or the family I remember from long ago when Dad was alive. Of course, ours was a more sedate rendition. Mom would die if this many *F* bombs blew up around our house.

I grab a fork and knife off the countertop, stab a plain dinner-plate-sized pancake, and drop it on an empty plate. My fork hovers over the second stack. Not sure what fruit is in there.

"Fresh blackberries," Rose says proudly, guessing at my hesitation. "I can still find a few patches around here. Kids and I like to pick."

There used to be wild blackberries growing all over our property. It makes me sad they're gone. My eyes rove to the fruit pancake pile again.

The hell with it. I stab a fruit pancake and lather it all in real butter, pouring maple syrup over the whole load.

Wring watches my movements like a hawk sighting prey. I'm almost too hungry and strung out with fatigue to care. Almost.

I find a seat at the kitchen table and plop down, digging in. As I chew my food, I look out the huge windows at the view of Kent from the top floor of the condominium complex.

I groan over the taste and close my eyes. *Heavenly.* A stab of guilt takes me out of the moment. Mom would love these. She's so skinny. The RA has stolen her appetite and dampened her sense of smell and taste.

"Like that sound," Wring comments quietly at my elbow, and I startle, my eyes snapping open.

My face heats. I set down the fork and put my hands to my cheeks.

"Hey," he says, voice low, "I didn't mean anything by that."

I can hear Rose clanking dishes in the background. It's just me and Wring.

Our gazes lock. "Yes you did." Defiance laces my words.

He nods really slowly. "You're right. I did."

My blush flares to life again.

Wring turns, digging into his own pile.

I watch him eat for a few seconds, then laugh.

One of his pale-blond eyebrows shoots up. "What?"

Eyeing up his six-pancake stack, I ask, "Hungry?"

He nods. "Fuck yes, starved. Feel like I just woke up after a ten-year nap."

Noose comes around the corner, securing Aria in a football hold at his side. "What nap? You sleep like shit."

Aria's chubby feet dangle, and she giggles. Noose chucks her underneath her chin, tipping her upright and high against his hip. Her arms curls around his beefy shoulder.

Wring runs a hand over his short buzz cut. "Yeah. Feel good right now, though."

"'Cause you just pounded that Blood." He shrugs like it's obvious.

They grin and tap knuckles across the table.

I take another bite then chase it down with icy orange juice.

"So spill it," Nooses says, eating a quarter of a pancake in one bite.

Wow, he's aggressive with the food.

Rose approaches the table, smirking.

Noose breaks off a little bit of pancake and pops it in Aria's mouth.

"Num-num!" she yells into the feasting.

I laugh. "She's adorable."

Rose beams, and Noose says to her, "You're welcome," dragging Rose in for another kiss.

She whacks him. "I had *something* to do with it, you know."

Noose winks. "Oh, I know. I *so* know."

"Noose…" she says in warning.

He ignores her, pulling her into his lap. "Great food, wife."

Rose's cheeks get pink, and he feeds her a bite from his fork, kissing her again as Aria scoops up a second tiny section of pancake. Her hair is dark, but her eyes are like her dad's, light gray. Syrup gets all over her chubby fingers.

"Ah, she's a mess, Noose," Rose chides.

He shrugs a muscular shoulder, his leather vest creaking with the movement. "She's a baby. They're dirt magnets."

"Amen," Wring says, cleaning the last of the syrup from his plate with a half pancake.

Rose sighs, getting up, and Noose slaps her butt. "Love the view, babe."

She gives him a long-suffering look, but underneath that is happiness. Rose loves him.

Noose turns back to me like a dog with a bone, steepling his fingers underneath his chin. "Why's that Blood prick after you?"

He gives Aria a little bit more pancake without missing a beat.

She mashes it between her fingers and stuffs it into her mouth. "Num-num!"

Both men stare holes through me. "I don't want to involve you in my..." I struggle for a few seconds to explain and finally settle on simple. "Troubles."

"Too late," Wring says, mopping up one last drop of syrup and grabbing his glass of OJ. He swallows half a glass, and I watch his powerful, thick throat work.

God, he's a handsome man.

He wipes his mouth with a napkin then crumples it before tossing it on the plate.

My heartbeats stack, my body flat out responding to his.

Wring watches my face and leans forward, pupils dilating. His lips part.

I concentrate on his mouth, sliding my damp palms underneath my thighs.

"Yeah," Noose agrees slowly. "Road Kill mess right now."

I turn to him in a semi-daze, food coma and lust undertones coming on. "What? Road Kill?"

He nods slowly. "We're motorcycle club men, Shannon." Noose says the words like they hold weight or mean something I should know.

I look to Wring.

The room seems to be holding its breath.

"I don't know what motorcycle club means." I lift a shoulder. "Like what? You guys like riding together?"

Noose starts braying like a donkey.

Wring doesn't join in.

"This is fucking rich," Noose says, slapping a denim-encased thigh with his hand.

"Cut the shit, Noose," Wring says, glaring.

"What am I missing?" I divide my attention between the two.

"Wring here"—he flings a thumb in Wring's direction—"went all white knight and shit, saving you from whatever that Blood had in mind." He tilts his head, clearly waiting for a response.

That's true. I nod.

"So the Bloods are going to look at that whole little event as a declaration of war. Unless you are someone important to Wring?"

I vigorously shake my head. "I don't know Wring." It occurs to me in that moment they have really weird names.

Wring leans back in his chair, carefully lacing his fingers. He cups the back of his head, hooded eyes on me.

I risk a look at his crotch. I don't know why. Because I'm crazy. Or curious. Both.

There's a healthy erection seated between his legs.

I squeeze my eyes shut. *Oh my God.*

"Wring?" Noose asks, and I manage to open my eyes and keep them on his face this time.

His expression is amused.

He knows I was checking his dick out. I about die. I'm blushing so hard, I feel like my head will explode.

"I don't want an old lady. Hell, I want easy tail."

I blink.

Noose chuckles, beginning to drum his fingers on the table. "That's what I thought, too."

"Num-num!" Aria chimes, and Noose slides another piece of pancake onto her tray. She makes a fist, squishes the pancake and syrup into an unrecognizable ball, and crams it into her tiny mouth.

"Tail?" I ask, feeling outraged. I stand, looking down on two amused faces and a startled baby. "I—ah!" I pivot on my heel and stomp out of there, intending to find Rose.

And where is Charlie?

I walk to where I hear faint voices, escaping their dumb conversation about old ladies, *tail*, and gangs.

Idiots.

Rose and Charlie are sitting together on his bed. A half-eaten plate of pancakes lies between them.

"Hey," she says softly. She sits up, reading my expression and getting kind of alarmed.

"Where's Aria?"

"She's out there, getting stuffed with pancakes."

"What's wrong?"

So much is wrong. I open my mouth to tell Rose some of it, realize I don't know her, and decide against it.

"The guys are so…" I waffle my hand back and forth.

"I know exactly what you mean." She kisses Charlie as he eats the rest of the pancakes and stands. "Time for Aria's nap."

Of course. Because my story hour was supposed to be at ten. And now it's almost one, and I can't—

My mom.

Fear goosebumps spread over my flesh. I wonder if Vincent tried to go by the house?

"What?" Rose asks, searching my features.

I look into her big brown eyes. Eyes that have seen a few things.

"I better get home," I say in weak response then remember my manners. "Thanks for the breakfast."

Rose grabs my arm as I move to turn.

I look at her.

"I know Wring—all of it, them—seems tough."

A laugh bursts out of me. *No shit.*

She studies my expression, and her face turns rueful. "But they—MC men, *our* MC men—they're real guys. Treat women well. Protective. Wring won't let anything happen to you."

I shake my head. I'm sure I look as puzzled as I feel. "I think it's great he helped me out," I say slowly. I put my wounded hand on my chest and cringe from the pain the movement fires off. "But he isn't responsible for me. *I'm* responsible for me." I spread my fingers over my chest and suddenly wince at the motion. I finally give up and let my mess of a wrist fall to my side.

"Oh my God." Rose covers her mouth. "Did that Blood do that to your wrist?"

I hold out my hand and really look it over. It's swollen, the little bone that normally pokes out where my hand and wrist connect is hidden in the inflamed flesh. "Yeah." A weary exhale slides out of me.

No health insurance. I'll just have to ride it out. I close my eyes. Tired over the challenges, taking care of my mom, and finances. Now this.

"I was going to take her to Doc."

I whirl. Wring's there, leaning against the doorjamb, looking tantalizing.

"I'm going home."

"No you're not. I'll take you by the club, get ya patched up, see what's what with your wrist, then you go home."

His eyes are flint, unyielding.

I fold my arms, thrusting a hip out—body language for digging in my heels. "I can say no."

We stare at each other.

He slowly nods. "You could."

I shrug, and it pushes my breasts up. His eyes cling to the view. Something deep and low pulls inside me at that look.

Wring's smile is secretive. "I highly suggest you don't."

5

WRING

"I don't need to be seen by a doctor."

I sweep my palm behind me, and Shannon sighs, hiking her leg over the seat and sliding in behind me.

Grabbing her hand before she can protest, I gently rotate it. Finger-shaped bruises ring the narrowest part of her arm. It's a mess, flesh inflamed. Looks like she couldn't use it if she tried.

"You're gettin' seen. Period."

I carefully place her wounded hand around me, and she tightens around my torso with her forearm but grips me with her other unhurt hand.

"Hang on," I say gruffly. *Bitches never listen.*

She lays her head between my shoulder blades like she's tired. "I—can we go by my house first? I have to check on my mom."

Hmm. Not real independent. Still lives with Mommy. I fight my irritation.

I guess she couldn't be perfect. Whatever, I didn't want complicated anyway. Got her away from the Blood dick. Get her seen by Doc. Get her the fuck home and out of my life.

Hell, even got her to eat something. I do like thin chicks, but a little meat on their bones can't hurt.

Shannon is too thin.

"Fine," I clip.

She tenses. "I don't want to be a bother. I just have to check on her."

I don't say anything, walking my bike backward out of the stall. I turn it on and gun it out of the underground parking area. "Where?"

Shannon tells me.

I just about upend the bike. *That place?*

I ask twice.

She replies pretty clearly.

Okaaaay.

Five minutes later, I'm pulling up into the driveway of the small faded old house I'd just thought was in the strangest place in all of Kent.

Deeply shadowed between two commercial highrises, it has a tiny garage that probably was once a carriage house for horses. A narrow front yard holds bright flowers behind a picket fence that's gray in spots. Its old white paint bleeds into the fissures of the decaying wood, giving it a bleached appearance.

There's a slight upward grade to the concrete drive-way, and we roll up there. I park then turn off the ride.

Shannon taps my shoulder then dismounts. With a little smile and wave, she begins to walk away. The small gesture of both thanks and temporary goodbye makes something deep inside me shift.

Fuck.

I don't know if I can let her go, this girl who lives in a shitty little house crammed between these buildings.

My eyes follow her, taking in the legs sticking out of the skirt, the low-heeled shoes, and the blouse.

She would look so hot in the stuff I have in mind.

I watch her until she's safely inside, then light a smoke. I inhale deeply and shoot the smoke into the air, thinking that stress and smoking go together. The two *S*s.

I chuckle, folding my arms. Looking way up at the buildings, I remember something. I swing my leg over the seat and take in the colorful graffiti running along the concrete bulkhead that borders both buildings, ending abruptly at Shannon's property line.

At first glance, it looks exactly like what it should. Art. Graffiti isn't unlawful everywhere anymore. Good old Kent decided to embrace it here. But hidden in the colorful swaths of bubble letters and rainbow artifice are the skillful tags of the Bloods.

See our territory? those symbols hidden in plain sight ask.

Road Kill's seen them. Read them. Knows what they mean for the club.

My gaze travels again to Shannon's battered little house. The front windows sparkle like good-humored eyes. I peer closer. There aren't any weeds in the flowerbed. The front door has a fresh coat of paint, and the gutters are clean.

I chuckle again, not that there's any debris to clog. The damn buildings flanking her place don't allow much from nature.

I suddenly sit up ramrod straight, flicking my cig on the ground and tramping it down with the toe of my boot. That's why that Blood is after her.

Shannon's house stands between two Blood buildings. Sure, they look legit. That's why they're here—trying to get some place that makes their shit seem aboveboard. Actually, they would like to make a new place as seedy as the old one.

Fuckers.

What I can't figure out is why she wouldn't get the hell out of here when the worst gang in the four-state area is nipping at her heels.

Shannon that stubborn? A smile spreads on my face. *I like 'em feisty.*

She opens the door, exiting the front. Her face is relieved. I can see it even though she stands in profile.

Shannon uses four locks on the door.

Oh yeah, she knows how dangerous continuing to live here is.

As she walks over to me, I notice she took the time to change.

Tight jeans hug her small body, and her long-sleeved T-shirt, a deep-green color, is just as tight. Black short boots are on her feet. Gone are the librarian clothes. Thank fuck. They were not sexy. Not that Shannon has to be sexy.

Yeah, she does. My chin sinks, and I hide my smile. She grabs the leather jacket she borrowed from Rose and shrugs it on. It just about works. Except across the chest.

Rose has got the biggest tits. Shannon's still look pretty fucking perfect to me.

"What?" she asks defensively, then her face tightens as she struggles to get the other sleeve of the leather on.

"Let me do it," I say and walk to her.

"No." She stumbles back. "I got it."

"Not gonna hurt you, Shannon."

Her eyes flick to mine then away. "I know." The empty sleeve dangles off her shoulder, and she cradles her hurt wrist against her chest.

"I'm not that Vincent prick. If you recall, I'm the one that gave him the little knuckle face dance, and I fed you. Technically, Rose fed you—had you meet some of my people."

Her lips quirk, and she looks at me, nodding quickly. "I know."

Awkward silence stands between us. I exhale in an irritated rush. "Then what's the fucking problem?"

She twists her hands then cries out.

A crack starts inside me from that sound, and I take her good hand, pulling her against me.

Shannon resists, putting her good arm between us. The sleeve flops around.

I wrap her against me, tucking her head underneath my chin. She's just barely short enough to do it, but I mash her against me.

"Stop fighting whatever this is."

"What is it?" she asks softly. Fragile.

"Fuck if I know. I'm just a guy that saw another dude rough you up. Didn't like it." I lift my shoulder, arms still securing her against me.

"So I could have been any female, and you would have pulled over and taken care of it."

I think about her words. I'm an honest guy. Gets me into trouble. Some might call me "brutally honest," but it's just who I am.

"Most," I admit.

She struggles from underneath my chin, and my stubble captures loose strands of platinum hair the quick braid she did before coming back out.

"So I'm nothing special?"

Not yet. I cup the back of her head for one second then step away. "No."

Shannon smiles, looking relieved.

Pisses me off.

I turn away from her and speak as I walk toward my ride. "Let's ride. Get ya to the club and then you can go home."

"Okay."

She slips in behind me, and her body feels right. Like she's always been at the back of my ride, against me. Like she's a piece of me I've been missing.

I know it's bullshit.

Shannon is just another sweet butt in prissy clothes. I'm never going to have what Noose and Snare have. That's fairytale shit.

And—I never believed.

I feel a tap on my shoulder and scowl. *What now?*

I crane my head around and look at her. Already pissed. She sort of rejected me. Crushed my autopilot mode I was just fine on.

"Wring?"

"Yeah," I reply, suddenly dying for a smoke. Or ten.

She touches my face briefly. "Thanks for helping me."

"Yeah," I turn around fast, chest tight. *Chicks.*

I roll out of there fast, not asking any more questions. Not giving a fuck.

Giving too many.

6

SHANNON

I cling to Wring's muscled back, trying to keep my mind on what's important. Figuring out my wrist. Then getting back to fix mom's supper.

When my thoughts turn to Vincent, I squeeze my eyes shut, and envision a future where he's skulking around every corner.

Not much of one.

I try not to think about how despondent it made me to hear Wring admit I was just a random woman in need of rescuing. But what did I expect? He's in some rival gang to the Bloods or whatever they are.

That still doesn't explain why Wring, by his own admission, took such a huge chance by stepping in where he clearly didn't belong.

Forget it, Shannon. He doesn't matter.

Figure out your priorities: Mom. Wrist. Job. God, *my job.*

I forget it all, trying to look around me and put my thoughts on a little-used shelf inside my tired brain. I don't dust the things I put there; I just push them to the back where they don't taunt me with their presence.

Wring takes me up West James Street, and we climb the roughly five hundred feet out of Kent Valley, the bike a warm rumbling presence between my thighs.

We cross Benson Street, now 515, and catch a rare green light just when we need it. He flies through, tempting the forty-five miles an hour speed limit.

When we get to 132nd and take a left, I lose track. After two more rights and a left, we roll down a long driveway and up to a huge old concrete building with windows really close to the roof.

Speaking of the roof.

I look up—way up. It has glass panels, similar to a greenhouse. I feel my brows come together. *Huh?*

When Wring turns off the bike, I wait. He pats my leg, and I have a pang of regret.

I've never ridden on a bike before Wring.

I've never had a man sacrifice for me. I'm no saint. I've dated—a lot. But once a man realizes I come as a package deal, they're out of here.

So I kind of gave up. On myself. On life.

Not that Wring would have been in the category of guys who would put up with Invalid Mom. It's almost enough to make me laugh.

Wring gets off after me, and I hand him the helmet he lent me. I give a little shiver. The bike is warm, the man is hot—but I'm not wearing a bike-riding outfit.

He gives me a lopsided grin, lifting his chin. "Helmet fits like shit."

I smile back. It was a little loose.

He puts his hands on his hips, seeming to think about something, glancing at the structure behind us. "It's Sunday, but there's some guys already here." Wring stops, and so do I. "This is our new digs. Nobody knows where we're at just yet, and we want to keep it like that." His serious eyes hold mine.

I lift a shoulder. "Of course."

"Stay by me, or the guys will hassle you."

I stop walking toward the door again. "Why? I'm not doing anything wrong."

He throws his head back, full belly laughing.

Not funny.

"You're gorgeous. And nobody's property, so yeah, sweet thing—they're gonna tag team you, Shannon."

I can feel my lips purse. "Tag team?"

He sighs, passing his palm back and forth over his hair in frustrated swipes. Wring walks slowly toward me, and I fight not to back up. He's all menace. And even though Wring doesn't direct it at me, it's clearly a part of who and what he is.

He must see something on my face. "I'm not gonna hurt ya." He sounds insulted.

I nod, meeting his bright azure eyes. "I know. But I-I had a scare today, and my wrist hurts and…" I study my scuffed old boots. "Maybe I don't have a job anymore," I end quietly.

I bite my lip and duck my head against my chest, trying to gather whatever remaining fortitude I have, forcing myself not to lose it in front of this man. "And I don't want to be 'hassled,'" I whisper.

Strong hands grip my shoulders. "Shannon, look at me."

Slowly, I lift my face and look into a gaze that rivals the blue of the Caribbean seas. Staring into his face, I know it would be so easy to forget the package of violence Wring represents.

His fingers clasp my chin loosely. "I know this isn't your world, and I'm sorry, but it's mine. I love the club, and I'm taking you here to get fixed up, and then you can go back to whatever citizen's existence you live." His astute eyes search my face, missing nothing. "But it wouldn't be right to just throw you to the wolves in there. These guys won't hurt women, but they sure like fucking, and you're just fresh meat to them."

I blink, and the first traitorous tear crawls down my face like a bloated, hot slug.

His face goes hard. "Don't fucking cry."

I shake my head, and more fly off my face. "Can't seem to help it." I suck in a breath, feel like I'll hyperventilate, and hold my breath.

My vision swims.

"Whoa—shit!" Wring hugs me. "Don't worry, Shannon, nobody's going to touch you in violence here."

"I can't stand it anymore, Wring. I'm sorry. You've just caught me at a bad time." That strikes me as funny, and I start laughing. Can't stop.

Wring holds me through my crying, snotting, laughing meltdown.

When I'm through, he steps away. "You gonna be okay?"

I look at him for a full minute. Finally, I nod. "I think so."

He takes my hand, and I let him, remembering his words that I wasn't anything special.

Good to know.

Wring wasn't kidding about the reception I would receive.

Speculative eyes roam my form as Wring and I walk through a crowd of bikers and scantily clad women. Ice clinks in glasses filled with booze before noon, and loud music blasts from four corners where Bose speakers are attached up high on the wall.

It appears as though construction just wrapped for the interior. A staircase leading up to the second floor has only particle board treads, naked of carpet or wood. Maybe the first floor is finished and the second isn't?

A large man moves toward us like a locomotive, and instinctively, I move behind Wring.

"Yo, Wring, my man!" His eyes are a striking blue, deeper than Wring's, and his hair is jet black. A cruel scar bisects his face.

He and Wring tap knuckles, then the other guy grabs him, hugging him and clapping him hard on the back. His eyes take me in over Wring's shoulder and narrow contemplatively. "Who's the sweet butt?"

I'm *really* beginning to hate that term.

Wring smirks. "Nah, man, it's not like that."

He peers around Wring and gives me steady eyes. He's huge, like the rest of them, but his eyes are kind.

"Ah-huh. So what's her story?"

"Later, Snare." Wring's voice tells the guy not to push.

Snare grabs his chest like he's having a heart attack. "Are you *dismissing* my ass?"

Wring smiles crookedly. "Yup." He pulls me after him.

Snare plucks at my sleeve, catching my bad wrist, and I hiss.

Wring whirls, grabbing Snare by the collar, and I stumble backward.

"Don't touch her."

Snare's eyes widen. "Hey, ya dicklick, I got Sara, you fucking 'tard."

I hold my injured hand against my chest. The room's sudden silence is deafening.

"What. The. Fuck?" Snare says. "Get your hands off me."

Wring tosses his hands away Snare, looking embarrassed, pissed, and unsure. It's a look I'm sure he doesn't wear too often.

"I'm sorry, he—Snare?" I ask a question at him, and he gives a quick nod. "He accidentally touched my wrist." I give a little shrug, and my face heats as everyone inside the club focuses on me. I want to crawl underneath something.

Snare gets to the heart of everything quickly. "Let me see."

I raise my hand, holding my breath as he touches my wrist and flips my hand over.

I breathe through the pain.

His eyes meet mine, filled with a knowledge I didn't give him. "What guy did this?"

My brows come together. "How do you—"

He shakes his head.

"I know."

"Fucking Blood," Wring says in both answer and explanation.

Shouting erupts, making me jump.

"Crips!"

"Fucking gang bangers!" From my left.

I cover my ears, and the noise goes away.

Suddenly, Wring is there, his eyes on mine. "Shannon."

I nod.

He looks at Snare. "Getting Doc to see her."

Snare asks, "How'd you happen to be Johnny-on-the-spot?"

Wring's lips twist, and he's handsome again. Heartbreakingly handsome. My hands drop, my wrist howling at being used.

"Just lucky, I guess." His hand rises to tuck a stray hair behind my ear.

I gulp back a wave of tears caused by the unexpected gesture. *What's wrong with me?* I guess I'm so freaked from Vincent and all the…whatever this is turning into.

"Yeah," Snare says, but not like he agrees. He backs away from Wring. "Well, I'll leave you to it, you temperamental flyaway fucker."

Wring gives a sheepish grin. "Sorry, brother, don't know why I flew off the handle like that."

Snare smirks, opening his mouth to speak.

"Don't say it if ya wanna live," Wring warns.

I want to know in the worst way what Snare would've said.

"Doc just came in. You got lucky."

Naked relief crosses Wring's features.

Probably can't wait to get rid of me.

"Great, let's go."

I let him drag me to the back and through a door marked with a medical symbol—sort of. It has a silver naked lady right underneath it. Someone's got a sense of humor. But I'm not laughing.

I walk in behind Wring, and a man is perusing something on his laptop, scouring something pretty thoroughly.

"Doc, shut off the porn. I've got a real live patient."

Oh God.

The man looks up, flustered, and shifts his weight, quickly closing the laptop.

Gross.

He stands, and I keep my eyes on his face.

Doc's on the good side of sixty, with spindly arms and legs and a jolly Santa Clause belly. He kind of reminds me of a human spider, but like Snare, he has compassionate eyes.

"Okay, what do we have?"

Wring points his jaw at the guy, indicating I should move forward. I stay put. "I don't have any medical insurance."

Wring gives me a curious look, and Doc says, "You showing up with Wring is the only insurance payment I need." He chuckles.

I inhale deeply, and without moving forward, I lift my hand, but he doesn't touch it right away. After a full minute, his voice is void of emotion when he asks quietly, "You staying with the man who did this?"

Heat suffuses my cheeks as I give a decisive shake of my head. "He—I was attacked."

"She's not gonna be hurt anymore," Wring growls, and Doc's graying eyebrows pop.

I whip my face to Wring, suddenly angry. "Don't make promises you can't keep. Vincent wants what I have. It's my mess. You got me out of there, and I'm thankful. But I think you and I both know he'll be back."

Quiet descends.

I understand I just made things weird between us, but I had to say the words. If I'm nobody special—and I *shouldn't* be—then his responsibility is null and void after he drops me off at my house today.

Finally, Wring nods. "You're right. I'll let Doc look at you, and then you can go home."

He's releasing me. It's the right thing to do. *So why do I hate the feeling that this is it?*

Doc moves gentle fingers over my wrist, and on two places he touches, I cry out. "Hurts," I whisper between clenched teeth.

He gives a disgusted exhale. "The guy strained her tendons. Badly. Going to need a brace."

My heart races. I can't afford that. *Gah!*

Doc's friendly eyes find mine, clearly reading a lot in my expression. "It's okay. Settle down. I've seen down and out. Hell, I've been there myself. Let us help you. You don't owe me nothing."

I nod. The muscles of my shoulders and back are stiff from me trying to hold my wrist still. I'm getting tired in a hurry.

He wraps my wrist, and I suck in shallow breaths as the ACE bandage wrap tightens over the bone. He proceeds to hand out meds like candy. I read the label. Great meds. I know because of Mom. Our house is practically a pharmaceutical store.

"These go for a boatload of dough on the street." His eyes slim on me. "Don't get hooked," he warns without a pause, "and take with food." His expression says he clearly doesn't think I eat.

Doc's sharp.

"Okay. Thank you." I grab the bottle of pills with my right hand. My left feels like a lead-encased club.

"Two weeks. Minimum. Come back here, and we'll check it."

His eyes move to Wring's. "Wrist can't go through that again. Not without some permanent damage." He scowls. "You know who did this, Wring?"

Wring nods. "Yeah."

"Good," Doc replies as if that closes things up.

It doesn't for me. Their information loop didn't include me, and I thought we'd just gone over how unspecial I was.

"Let's go," Wring says to me and walks out of the office.

I hug the Doc. Porn surfer or not, he patched me up.

He hugs me back. "Be careful, Shannon."

I nod and turn quickly, jogging after Wring. Catcalls and whistles follow me, even with my sexy club hand.

Wring whirls, and I bounce into his chest. When he steadies me with a strong hand, I swear my stupid heart flutters.

"No," he points at the general group of guys, and they shut up.

"This is Shannon."

I raise my good hand, but their eyes are on my bad one.

"She's not to be fucked with."

Eyes move over my body then swing to Wring's serious features.

"Whatever, brother," one guy says from the shadows.

Wring scowls, and I creep a little closer to him. "Just as long as we're fucking crystal clear. You won't be seeing her around anyway."

My gut twists at his words, but I know they're true. I look down at my feet.

Assent is voiced all around.

The guy from the corner says nothing as he and Wring stare each other down.

Finally, Wring walks out without a word.

I follow, knowing this is my last bike ride. I'm happy for the day to be almost over—and sad for reasons I don't look too closely at.

7

WRING

Fucking women.

The one at my back is giving me an epic boner. Her. *Shannon.*

I wanted to kill men who are my brothers—men I would die for—because they were giving her an eye fuck as she jogged after me with her arm cast and cute ass.

If I admit it to myself, what I'm really pissed about is taking her home—and that I told her I would have rescued any chick in distress. That's only mostly true.

But Shannon's not any chick. I don't know how I know. I just do. It's like when I would hear a twig snap in the night and know it was the wind. Or when it was the enemy. I just knew.

Like I know now.

I cruise as slowly as I ever have. Late-Sunday traffic is nothing to navigate. I use the familiar shortcuts people take in this shitty town where the roads and streets weren't thought out and drivers have to fucking screw around on all the back roads just to get from point *A* to point *B*.

When I hit Kent Station, I take a left into the meat of the area. People are scattered around the train depot, but traffic isn't heavy the way it usually is, so I take the reverse direction toward Noose's place.

I pass Top Shelf and keep heading north. Shannon squeezes my body with her thighs, and I tense, fighting my body's reaction to her. To her nearness.

We glide past where that fucker hurt her, and her arms tighten around me. But the place is empty of action and people. A few more blocks, and we arrive at her house again. She taps my shoulder, and I nod.

When she dismounts, I grab her good hand, helping her down.

Goosebumps cover her arms, even though she borrowed Rose's spare leather jacket.

I lick my lips, wanting to warm all that exposed flesh. My eyes rise to meet hers, and Shannon's are sad. I put my hands on my thighs to keep from comforting her.

Touching her.

"Thanks again."

I don't look at her. "I'll come back in a couple of weeks, swing ya by Doc's, and see how you're healing up."

"Okay."

Between us, the engine ticks, cooling. I'm hyper alert to the possibility of the Bloods visiting while it's just me here. Or just her.

I gotta know. "Why is this Blood hassling you?" I tear a palm over my skull and try to ask a rational question, "Why do you know him?"

She laughs, and the sound has a hysterical edge to it. I swing my head in her direction, sharpening my gaze on her.

The wind kicks up, and she shivers. Sometimes, late August into September is cool. The easterly usually blows warm. Not today.

I study my fingers, taking note of the callouses from knotting. Working. Fighting.

I look up again, calming my shit. I don't own this girl. I have no right to any information she doesn't want to give up.

Shannon looks into the wind "It's been a couple of years now."

I wait, wanting a smoke pretty bad. *Fuck it.* I open up the pouch between the handlebars and reach in. Flipping the hard box lid open, I bring it close to my mouth then flick a cig out the top and catch it between my lips.

Nasty little habit, I think—until the first drag calms my fraying nerves.

Shannon doesn't seem to notice. "I didn't know who he was. Just another thug that doesn't wear pants that fit." She gives a pathetic laugh.

I snort. She looks at me, and the expression on her face has my smile fading.

"He and his friends—"

"Gang members," I say.

She nods. "Yes. He and his thug friends kept coming by the house, and I'd notice their traffic patterns. Same time of day. Looked like a habit was forming. I phoned the police."

I sit up straighter at that.

Damn.

She sucks in a deep breath before letting it out in an irritated rush. "The cops said people have a right to walk around."

Her eyes meet mine. "Then I found out the gang owned the buildings." Shannon points to the buildings on either side of her small red house.

"The first time they knocked on my door..." She shudders and looks at me. Shifting her weight, she looks away. "They scared my mom."

Her throat moves as she swallows past the memory. "They scared me."

Fuck.

I get off the ride, suck a last drag, put the cig out on the tread of my boot then stuff the butt in a small cup I keep inside my pouch.

Shannon holds up her hand. "Don't."

I stop. I wasn't going to do anything. Right? My eyes move down her body.

Right.

"Anyway, he told me his name was Vincent, and they'd buy our house."

My eyebrows rise then come together. "How much?"

"Two-fifty."

I whistle. "Not bad, really?"

She exhales, and pale-blond strands of hair float around her face like displaced angel hair. "That's the *money* part of the offer."

Ah.

My hands fist. I want to beat that fuck. Hard. My fingers burn for the knots that have his name on them. Vincent.

"He said I could be…" She covers her face with her hands. "His personal bitch," she whispers between her fingers.

"Nope."

Her face turns to me. "What?" She clears her throat, wiping at tears she just realized were on her face. "What do you mean 'nope'?"

I smile, and it's the first real one of the day.

"God—your face."

Yeah, my face. "Why didn't you take the deal?" *I've gotta know.*

She bows her head, her blond hair turning to the color of blood with the setting sun.

"I can't. My mom is dying. She shouldn't be moved. I don't want her to be taken from the only home she's ever known."

I slide my jaw side to side. *Hell, shit's complicated.*
Figures. "What's wrong with her?"

Her eyes flick away. "She's got rheumatoid arthritis."
"Joint bullshit?"

She sighs. "Yeah, something like that. Listen,
Wring…" She begins to walk away, and I follow her.
Nobody walks away when I'm talking to them, and I
grab her, swinging her around.

Shannon yelps, putting her hand against her chest.
"I'm tired, and I'm frustrated. I know Vincent will be
back, and now I'm even more defenseless. The meds my
mom has taken so she can move normally have ruined
her body. So now—she doesn't have much time. And this
gang loser just wants to take what little bit we have and
use me in the process."

I know she's saying words, explaining what's wrong,
why she's in this mess.

But I'm mesmerized by her lips. I want to taste them.
Wrapping an arm around her, I pull her in close.

I'm so fucked up. My needs. My want.

Shannon's mess is just secondary. Once I get us
worked out, I'll clean shit up. Clean up her disaster.

"What—"

Then my mouth is on hers.

I think she's so startled that she doesn't know what
to do.

But I know what to do. I lift her with my arm, walk
her to the small entryway, and push her up against the

wall. Shadows swallow us whole. My knee goes between her legs, automatically seating underneath her pussy through her jeans.

"No," she says with a husky catch, but she's kissing me back.

Generally, I ignore words and listen to a chick's body. Shannon hooks her heels around my calves, and I lift her up by small ass cheeks and press her slender body into mine. My cock fits right where it meets her most tender part.

"Tell me to let you go." I kiss her throat, licking a long hot line from earlobe to collarbone, and she shivers. "And I will."

"Why?" she breathes.

"Don't know. I'm so fucking hot for you, I'm going to blow. Tried to ignore it. Can't."

"I won't do this," she says against my mouth as her hips press against my raging hard-on.

I pull away, pinning her body with my knee, and rest my hands on either side of her head. We're still kissing close, but I'm not doing that soft shit anymore.

I won't be fucking played. Can't afford to be. I'm a fucking menace. To her.

To myself.

I can't even fucking catch enough z's to goddamned think.

She searches my face. "I don't know what that look means, but it scares me."

I stroke her jaw. "It should. I'm a fucking hard man, Shannon. Harder than that little stroke Vincent could ever pretend to be."

She nods. "I know."

"You don't. You don't know anything about me."

She leans forward, touching her forehead to my shoulder, and something tight unbinds inside me. "I know one thing," she states quietly.

My heart thunders, and I stay still, trying to get control of my shit. "What do you *think* you know?"

Her hands creep around my neck, small fingers lighting on my skin like licks of fire. "You're the man who protected me."

Fuck.

"I didn't want to," I admit. Like just seeing her somewhere, deep down inside, I knew she'd change shit.

"Then why did you?"

I groan, sidestepping her question and pulling on her mouth with a sucking press of lips and tongue. Shannon responds, cradling my face with her hands and kissing me back.

"I don't know."

My confession sits uncomfortably between us. Finally, she squirms and gasps, eyes flying wide and pinning my gaze.

I grin. "Knee's in the right place."

She blushes. "I suppose it is."

I press upward, and she grips my shoulders. "Wring—I can't."

"You keep saying that shit, then you keep rubbing one out on my kneecap."

"Oh God. The way you talk."

I didn't think skin could turn that red. I stroke a finger over her hot flesh. "You like the way I talk?" I ask softly.

She nods, ducking her chin, not meeting my eyes.

Well, *damn*.

I gently lower her to the ground, my face tightening when I see her wrist wrapped in that fucking bandage.

Pulling a knuckle over her collarbone, I watch the blush slide after the touch, soft pink color rising underneath the slide of my finger.

She grabs my hand. "Wring," she says softly, and I look into her eyes. "I don't need a boyfriend, or anyone else."

"I'm not a boyfriend."

Shannon inches her body from between me and the wall. "What are you?"

I swallow everything I'm feeling, cramming it deep down inside. These new feelings? They don't mean dick.

"Nobody." I turn around and walk back to my bike, taking my time. I turn it on, flip on my brain bucket, and begin to roll out backward.

When I look up, Shannon's gone.

And that cavernous empty spot inside me grows bigger.

8

SHANNON

After unlocking the four locks on the outside of the house, I slip inside.

The powerful engine of Wring's bike grows more distant. I shut the door, blocking out the motor.

I turn, placing my palms flat on the door, and try to forget that moment in the entryway.

It's harder than it should be.

I rotate around slowly.

Mom sits in the gloom. The small lamp she reads by casts a soft glow and shadows throughout the space.

Her face rises from her book, and she smiles. Then Mom takes in my disheveled outfit, and something in my face must tell her.

"What is it, darling?" she asks.

I duck my head, hiding the quivering of my bottom lip. *Wimp*, I chastise myself. "I had a tough day." *Understatement of the year.*

"I'd say," she says with a wry twist of lips.

I jerk my head up at the tone in her voice.

"I saw that young man outside." Her smile remains.

Oh God. A blush flares to life, and I feel like my head will blow up.

"Mom, you're not supposed to run around."

She smooths her painter-style shirt over her wasted thighs. "I believe my days of running are long over."

I roll my eyes and fold my arms. "It's an expression."

"I'm aware, Shannon." Her lips purse. "Tell me what's bothering you."

"Did you go to the bathroom?" My gaze dives toward the walker at her left, leaning up beside the end table where it should be, and I see it's positioned slightly differently than I left it. I breathe out a sigh of relief.

"Yes"—she gives a small smile—"I accomplished that at least."

"I'm sorry."

"Stop apologizing and tell me what's happening. Don't shelter me. We've made a vow with each other—"

"To never lie or deceive through omission." My gaze locks with hers.

Mom's smile widens, and I remember, very vaguely, a time when she wasn't in pain every minute of every day.

I smile back.

"Exactly," Mom answers.

I inhale deeply. "You remember Vincent?"

Her brows meet. "The unmentionable?"

I laugh again, though it's not funny. "Yes, him. He's back," I admit on a shaky sigh.

Mom sets down the tea she was drinking, and I automatically check the thermos, wondering if it's still full of hot water. A small bowl next to it holds two used tea bags. "And?" she asks, sipping.

"He hurt me."

Mom sits up straighter, all pretense of forced calm gone.

I bring my injured wrist around to the front of my body. I know when her vision grabs onto the bandaged appendage.

"What did that horrible man do?" Her eyes, usually so gentle and compassionate, are blue ice chips in her face.

"He—he tried to get me to see his perspective."

"Oh, Shannon." Mom sets the cup down with a rough clank and dumps her face in her gnarled hands.

I rush to soothe her. "It's okay—for now. Wring happened to come by and saw...saw what Vincent was doing and stopped him."

Slowly, Mom lowers her hands and stares at me. "The bike rider?"

My lips quirk. Wring is so much more than that. But whatever he is, I don't know exactly what.

He's the man who rescued me from a guy who means me harm. And Vincent wants to make me suffer. Not because I've ever done anything against him—just because that's his way.

I shiver.

"You can't go to your job by foot anymore, Shannon."

"Mom!" I say, exasperated. "I need the money. *We* need the money. I can't hole up here and hope that he'll just go away. He wants our house."

Mom's lips become a flat line. "Is that all he wants?"

I look at my toes, thinking about my job. I sigh. I'll have to phone, do damage control.

What am I going to say? I can just hear myself now. "Yeah, Sally—there's this gang guy and he harasses me so he can make me his little whore and steal my mom's house. So sorry. Today, he just happened by and wrenched my wrist while a gang biker guy saved me and…" Yeah.

Aloud, I say, "No. It's not all he wants."

"Let's phone the police again." Mom spreads her fingers on her thighs.

I shake my head, biting my bottom lip. "That's not going to work. These guys are just smart enough to not get caught hassling me." I look into her face. "And you. What happens if they get really bold and break in here while I'm at work?"

Mom hikes the archaic phone that habitually rests on the table top beside her lamp and well-worn paperback. "I phone 9-1-1."

I hang my head. "Mom, they could hurt you before the police could respond."

"Maybe it's time for that state home, Shannon," Mom confesses in a low voice. "It's *beyond* time. Sell the house, give it to that thug; keeping our home is not worth our lives. Get what money we can and fund my care that way. You could get a proper job and have a degree of autonomy you've never had before."

I walk toward Mom and sink, resting my butt on the heels of my boots.

She searches my face, smoothing my hair back, and smiles. "I've robbed you of your life, darling."

I vehemently shake my head, afraid I'll cry if I speak.

But she holds my face with her crippled hand and tilts her head. "The disease has."

A sick exhale slides out of me. I can't dispute that fact. "Yeah."

"What does it matter if this Vincent gets the house? Let him have it for—what was it? Two hundred fifty thousand dollars? I could receive help; you wouldn't be in this never-ending cycle of caretaking." Her eyes search my face. "You could have a career with children. Like you've always wanted."

Her words fill my head like a dream.

Except the nightmare of Vincent isn't going to go away.

"I want that. I mean, if there was anyone who could take care of you the way *I'd* want it done."

Our rueful smiles match.

"Anyway," I say, putting my hand over hers, "he doesn't just want the house anymore, Mom. Maybe, if we'd said yes the instant he'd asked a couple of years ago, the deal would be done. Our home would belong to a gang member."

She gives a regretful sigh. "No one ever said life would be easy."

No shit.

"But now he wants me to be some kind of slut groupie or something." My laugh is sad even to my ears.

"Absolutely not." Mom gives an emphatic shake of her head.

I shrug, gently taking her hand inside my own. I turn it over, staring at the tissue-paper-thin skin covering slim blue veins. "I know. That's the thing. Now, it's personal." I search her face. "I can't agree to one without agreeing to the other."

Mom's smile is sudden, clever.

"What?" I ask, excited. She's thought of something. I know it.

"Let's just commit, Shannon—put the house on the market. It's zoned commercial. There's no reason why someone else wouldn't be interested."

Her eyes gleam with unshed tears. Instinctively, I know Mom would never sell our family homestead unless I was on the line. She's that stubborn.

But she's not stupid. And if I say the gang guy wants to make me part of some messed up harem, she'll do everything in her power to get me out of harm's way.

Unfortunately, I feel the same way about her. The two of us are a real pair.

"He'll know."

Mom's chin lift is defiant. "Ask me if I care." Her snow-white eyebrow, speckled with pewter, quirks.

"Do you care?"

Her smile is sure. "Not a fig."

We grin. "Okay, maybe we can get the place sold quickly. We grab the money and run. Get you full-time in-home care. I can get more hours at the library."

If they'll still have me.

"What is it?" she asks, and I'm too late to halt my expression. Mom's lips twitch. "I could always read you, darling. Every emotion you have shows on your face. You're very expressive."

That's the problem. Vincent knew I wasn't going to ever cooperate. I didn't have to tell him. He read it on my face.

Nothing wrong with that chode's street smarts. Except they're focused on me.

"By the time Wring helped me, I'd already missed reading hour."

Hot tears threaten, and I brutally beat them into submission. If Mom senses how distraught I am about all this, she might backtrack and try to take on more than she should.

"Your job? Pfft," she says dismissively. "Phone Sally, explain the incident with this ruffian. She'll understand. But don't wait."

I stand. "Can I help you to the bathroom? Get you a snack?"

Mom inclines her head back. "I'm *fine*. I've used the little girls' room and fetched some crackers and ginger ale. Take care of you, Shannon. Stop fussing."

Fussing. Yeah, that's me.

I begin walking away to call my boss.

"And I want to hear all about this new man. This biker."

I stop, turn. "There's nothing to tell."

There's so much to tell.

"I think that any man who would come between you and that hoodlum is better than most."

I nod. "He is, but I'm not ready for what he offers."

I'm actually judging Wring harder than my own mom is.

She frowns. "And what is that? Besides being a good Samaritan?"

I reply slowly, "Danger."

Mom chuckles and I frown.

"Don't be so quick to judge, Shannon," she says, echoing my thoughts.

The memory of him picking me up off the ground by my butt and hammering me against the wall with his mouth, splitting me with his dick, rises to the surface of my brain.

Unforgettable. No, I think my assessment of danger is right on target.

I need to stay away from Wring as much as possible.

But not because he's a physical danger to me. Instinctively, I know he would never hurt me.

He's a danger to me in a much greater sense. I face obsession, lust, and a whole shit ton of other risks.

Besides, he's made it clear I was just a female who needed saving.

Nothing more.

Or less.

"I appreciate you calling, Shannon. We were so worried. And your explanation of events is colorful."

Colorful. I can't stand Sally. She's so cloying and insincere. I swallow what little pride I can hang onto and kick off my boots. They tumble on their sides on the battered old wood floor. "Um, yeah. I was terrified."

Some gang guy about tears my hand off, and she's pissed because she had to do reading time on the fly.

Thank God I kept details vague, putting the entire encounter under "mugging."

I muffle my sigh of exasperation.

"I know you've been on the list for additional hours, but if you can't get to work on time with only the twenty-five hours we give you…"

I fill in her silence with the unseen shrug she gives.

"We're putting the house on the market." I pause for a few seconds, hating to confide in this bitch of a boss who has less than zero compassion. "If it sells quickly, my mom and I can afford in-home care, and I can take on more hours." My voice holds all the hope I feel.

A couple beats of time drum past, then she replies, "When that eventuality happens, we'll reassess your employment options. As it stands, you're on ninety days' probation starting now."

"Sally—"

"I'm sorry, Shannon. You're a great employee in many ways, but this inconsistency. What with your mother's illness—"

"RA," I say, with barely contained disgust.

"With her troubles," she corrects, going on, "you've missed or been late to work more times than we would normally tolerate. The City of Kent has high stan-dards of punctuality and attendance from employees. Appearances and professionalism are critical."

Scalding tears collect like a river of molten fire, beginning to run down my face.

Please, please don't fire me. I can't. I don't have enough money to hold me over before I get a new job, not to mention a job I love.

"You get one more chance, Shannon."

I cover my mouth then release a breath in a gust of relief. My fingers shake as I wipe the tears from my hot cheeks.

It kills me to say what I know I must. "Thank you, Sally."

"You're welcome. And I'd recommend relocating to a different neighborhood, where these sketchy types aren't around for you to encounter."

I don't correct her. It's no use. Sally won't understand or listen. She wouldn't believe me when I say I don't—and never would—hang around with gang members. Sally would never understand that my life revolves around taking care of my mom and bringing home whatever money I can in to keep surviving.

Sally's never been challenged with anything other than being a bitch to her underlings.

"Don't you agree, Shannon? That mixing with these types breeds trouble?"

I was not mixing.

I tighten my fingers on either side of my hips, crumpling my bedspread, holding my prepaid cell against my ear with my shoulder.

"Yes," I whisper.

"Excuse me?"

"Yes," I seethe.

I swear I can hear her smile. "Excellent. We'll see you tomorrow then."

"Okay."

"Goodbye."

I open my mouth to say goodbye, but there's just a void where she hung up on me.

Empty. Like my life.

I start to feel sorry for myself then squash those emotions. Self-pity is a luxury I can't afford.

Cruising my apps on my cell, I find a big local real estate company.

I call.

They're very receptive to our small house crammed into all-commercial zoning. Sure—they'll come by tomorrow afternoon after I get off work and survey the property.

A tired smile spreads over my face then fades as I realize what Mom and I have to give up more than a house—it's our heritage, too.

I soak my pillowcase with tears.

Sometimes, it seems like the decisions I have to make are the best choice among bad ones.

9

WRING

"Not good." Noose shrugs.

"Just find out, will ya?" I ask.

He gives me a hard stare. Actually, that's his normal look. "You'll check out my stock portfolio?"

I snort. "Tit for tat."

Noose binds his longish dirty-blond hair in a hair tie that roughly matches the buff color. "Fuck no. But with Rose and Aria—I need to have something to fall back on. Condo's paid for. Now I need to do something with the green—stash it. And I don't know how to play the market. I don't have the financial know-how. You feel me?"

I do. "Just giving you shit. I'll get your cash set up in some good companies."

Noose rolls his shoulders like they're tight. "'Kay. Just wanna look out for the family."

I smirk.

Too busy being pleased with myself to see Noose's fist.

I feel it, though, when it hits me in the arm, spinning me off the chair I was perched on. I hit the floor like a cat then tackle him around the legs.

"Fucker!" he howls.

Big lug lands on his back and snaps his hands around my neck.

Snare walks in and sees the two of us. Snorts. "What are you fucking Nancy's doing rolling around on the floor?"

Noose is strangling me, and I'm thinking about gouging his eyes out when Lariat sails in on Snare's heels.

"Dumb fucks, can't keep your hands off each other." He grunts and wades past Snare.

"Fucker," Noose seethes, fingers biting.

I hit him open handed in the face.

"Bring it, ya pussy."

Huh.

Lariat dangles a knot between us like a white flag of truce.

Fuck.

Noose lets go.

I rise, glancing at his crotch.

He smirks. "Rose'll kill you if you fuck with the jewels."

"Really?" I ask, thinking about a woman killing me because she can't have another man's cock in her anymore.

Now that's devotion.

"You think that's funny?" Noose asks, standing, looking pretty ragey.

"I do."

"Couple of cat-fighting girls."

"He started it." I point at Noose.

Snare folds his arms. "Like I was saying."

"What the fuck is going on?" Lariat looks between the two of us.

"Wring's being a dumb fuck about this chick, poking some fun at me because I'm all domestic and shit."

I glower, looking at my boots. I guess I'm pretty transparent. Especially to Noose.

"What's going on? Why do I come in here and you guys are beating the shit out of each other?" Lariat's dark gaze searches both our faces.

"He won't admit he's got it bad for this girl."

I look at Noose. "I only admit that I want to close the loop with her. I came by—wrong time, wrong place. This fucking Blood was hurting her, and…I don't know. Didn't fucking like it. Made him stop."

Lariat whistles. "*This* is why Viper's calling emergency church. He's going to want to hear all about it."

I hang my head. I endangered the club by interfering. All the delicate turf war establishment and domination might be ruined.

Snare studies my expression. "We've all done shit, Wring. What's going on?"

"What's going on is Wring has pussy fever, and along with not sleeping, he can't think until he taps this girl."

I whirl, grabbing Noose by the collar.

"Fuck," Lariat spits and slaps his palms on our napes, slamming are skulls together.

Noose sits on his ass, and I stagger backward.

"You two fucking children are going to get along."

We look at each other, and I press a hand to my head where Lariat knocked our shit together.

"I like tapping twats," I say slowly. "Nothing better. I sure as fuck don't need some girl that's got a fucked-up home situation with a chaser of gang."

Snare spreads his arms wide. "Yeah. That all sounds great in theory. You sleeping around—or just sleeping?"

I let my anger slide out on my next exhale, like a dragon breathing fire.

Snare chuckles. "But when there's a woman you can't stop thinking about, that usually means one thing."

"It's never just pussy when you can't stop festering over a chick."

"Why don't you fuck it out?" Nooses suggests with a shrug, hauling himself to his feet and spreading his arms away from his body.

I shake my head. "I could try, but the truth is, I'm concerning myself with her when she's not around.

Fucking sweet butts will only be a distraction from my goddamned issue."

"What?" Lariat asks in thinly veiled disgust. "You met this girl yesterday?"

I give a curt nod.

"You can't be feeling anything—hell, is this a white-knight complex or something? You know we're not in the sandbox anymore, right? We don't have to save everyone."

Noose and I look at each other then at Lariat. We tap knuckles like people toast with champagne.

"Ya can't save everyone, Wring," Snare comments quietly.

I fist my hands. "I don't want to save everyone."

"Just her," Noose guesses with unerring accuracy.

My head swivels in his direction. "Yeah, fucking genius. Just her."

I walk away.

Gotta go to church and get my ass chewed and spit out.

Viper leans back, drumming his fingers on the battered church table. His faded-blue eyes peg me where I sit.

We usually meet at eleven in the morning once per week. Why the late hour? Lots of hung brothers. And I don't mean in the cocky way, like horses. But hung from booze and bitches.

"I don't know, Wring. You're the most level-headed of all the brothers."

"Amen," says Storm, a prospect who has a knack for opening his mouth at the least opportune times. Noose glares at him, and he exhales in justified fear.

Noose grins at his expression. He gives Viper a swift look. "Vipe, Wring and I got into it."

"Heard. Ya dumb bitches, we don't have time for a beatdown among ourselves." He swings his finger between the two of us. "I need you guys to be ready for our enemies. What were you two lovebirds quarreling about anyway?" He rolls his eyes as though weary. "Gotta be pussy." His thick eyebrows rise.

Silence.

"Isn't it always?" Snare says out of nowhere.

"Yup," Lariat replies instantly, giving me a hard look.

I guess I earned that.

"Noose tells me you came between a Blood and his bitch."

I bristle. Shannon is *not* Vincent's bitch. But I want him to be mine. My hands still tingle from the memory of her under my skin.

Viper waits.

I form my answer carefully. "I was killin' road, on my way to Noose's for some food."

"Rose was making pancakes?" Trainer asks with a hopeful lilt.

I shut him up with a glance.

"Fine, fuck," he says in a sullen mumble.

I point at him. "You're lucky you're patched in, or you'd be on cum and piss patrol."

Trainer pulls a face of such pure disgust it cracks us up. When we've finally controlled ourselves I continue, "I was driving through Kent Station, saw a Blood manhandling a chick."

Viper's shoulder lifts in a clear *So?*

I rub a hand over my skull, feeling the bite of many short hairs needling my skin. "She didn't look like a working girl. I might have let it slide if I thought she was a Blood flesh worker."

"Hate those fucks. Drugging girls and putting them out on the street like turning out a cat on a stoop." Viper's hate thrums through his voice.

Lots of assent passes around the table.

"Love the bitches, but I'm for them having a choice of who they want to bang." Storm leans back in the chair, hands folded behind his head, eloquent as always.

I shake my head.

Noose tips Storm's chair back with a finger, and he falls backward, cracking like an egg on the floor, limbs scattered and tossed behind him.

He wails.

Noose grins as he and Lariat tap knuckles.

"Boys?" Viper says in a low voice of warning. Then he turns that Prez gaze on me.

There's a reason why he's the club president. He's steel, through and through. He's seen war. Close up. And a lot of other mind-numbing shit.

Like us knotters. Noose and Lariat are my brothers in the club. But we were brothers in war before we landed here.

Viper's got that kind of understanding, too.

"Anyway…" I cast a glare at Noose, and he flips me off, shooting me a tight smile. "I knew she wasn't a whore, so I slowed down."

"Why?" Noose asks.

Dick.

"She—fuck—she gave me a look, okay?" I toss out my words like throwing stars. Hoping, they strike any soft underbelly sitting here.

Hard eyes stare back, from hard men. There's no sympathy, only a need for answers.

"A fucking *look*?" Snare asks, incredulous.

I nod. "It was like she was speaking right to me." I cup my hand behind my ear. How could I ever forget those big green eyes pleading at me from the sidewalk?

"What was she saying?" Lariat's lips pull up.

Jesus, these fuckers.

"Help." My eyes blaze at Noose and Snare. They've got women. They know what I mean. "You know the look, Noose, right?"

He suddenly becomes interested in his hands.

"Right?" I roar into the sudden silence, and his chin jerks up.

"I don't want to scout this girl, if she's just some snatch you want to hump then dump." Noose shrugs.

"Have I ever asked you to check anything out?"

He shakes his head. "No, but let me tell you something, pal. When we were fighting together, you were fucking ice man. Nothing thawed your ass. You were the most neutral fucking human being I've ever known. So forgive me if you wanting me to intel some librarian girl is a little fucking *odd*."

Heat rises; my neck's a torch holding my head upright. I rub my nape, feeling how warm it is, then drop my hand.

"Okay." Viper holds up his hands. "We've established that this girl—" He waits.

"Shannon," I offer, and no one breathes a word. Better fucking not.

"Shannon, needs protection, but we also need to be fucking careful. This is Bloods here. And there's more of them than us. Even if our charters in Oregon and Idaho—and hell—Montana help, we're still fucked in the ass without lube, if this comes to an all-out war."

"I thought we were taking back turf?" Trainer asks in a serious voice.

Still hard for me to think of him as a brother, but god*damn* if he didn't do his time as a prospect.

"We are, but all our moves are like a waltz. We know the dance steps, and we're trying to lead reluctant partners."

"Pretty poetic, Viper," Snare says.

"Stick around. I can wax poetic if the mood strikes."

Chuckling all around.

I know what I've done has stressed the resources of the club and put us in a vulnerable position.

"What about that cop that's working undercover in Chaos?" Storm asks.

I frown.

"What about him?" Viper asks. "Can't do anything with that. We're all under wraps about his identity. He's still playing MC."

Everyone laughs. No one's got anything against the cops. Actually, we do, but we're saving it in case they get in the way of us dealing arms.

Otherwise, everyone's fucking hunky-dory.

"Just sayin'." Storm shrugs. "Thinking he might have some insight."

Prez hikes a brow, clear surprise reigning supreme on his face. "Um, that's a good point, Storm." He clears his throat, and it sounds like a grunt. "So, getting the cops involved in gang territory is never good." He strokes his chin.

"You throwing down for Blondie?" Prez asks.

I would hit anyone else for calling her that. "No," I answer in a short word. "I didn't come here for club support." I lean back in the chair, folding my arms. "I wanted intel. I knew Noose could provide it."

"You also knew that you were coming between Blood and pussy."

Fuck. "Yeah."

"So if you didn't think she mattered, and you knew what was at stake, it was poor judgement, at best?"

Viper gets to the heart of shit.

I crack my knuckles under the table. "Yes," I hiss.

"If she's your property..." Viper shrugs.

"I know what it is if she's my property. I don't need property." I direct the veiled insult at Snare and Noose but can't quite work up to disdain.

"Then we can't help you. If you throw down for Blondie..."

My flinty eyes capture his.

Viper chuckles. "You got it bad, you stubborn fuck. It's like a damn broken record. First, Noose loses his prick, then Snare—fuck, I'm getting too old for all the babysitting I have to do with you swinging dicks." He shakes his head.

"I haven't Lost. My. Dick," I say through my teeth.

"Yet," Storm says with a smile.

I stand.

Noose does, too, wagging a finger at me. "I already pushed him over in his chair for ya."

"I beat him up last year," Snare volunteers, and I slowly sit down again.

"Stay away from Blondie," Viper says. "Noose will look into why she's so attractive to Vincent. Because his interest doesn't seem to agree. Plenty of bitches love the gangbangers. He doesn't need this one. She's work." He chuckles. "But it seems like all the brothers don't take after simple."

I scowl.

"Yeah," Trainer says, sucking on a lollipop, making his tongue bright red, "it's like *Sesame Street*. What doesn't belong."

"You're fucked up," Storm says.

"I bet there's some shit for you to clean up," Trainer says conversationally.

Storm groans, and we laugh.

"He's right," Viper says.

All heads turn to him.

"Noose will find out why this Shannon is so interesting to the Bloods."

I know why. They want her home. Her. Noose isn't going to be finding out about that. I want to know about Shannon. The woman. Not the commodity.

That's why Noose is pissed.

If I would admit she's important to me, he would be looking already. But because I won't, he got pissed.

I can't admit that to him. If I do, then it's real.

10

SHANNON

The Realtor is a smarmy guy with slicked-back hair and perpetually pursed lips. His mouth is an angry line underneath a beaky nose.

But he came highly qualified. His real estate company is rated number one in the state. I heave a mental sigh.

"Maybe two hundred thousand," he sniffs, closing the drape over the window that faces the busy street.

Herman Humphries has already trudged with his expensive tie-up loafers across our diminutive backyard. An old cyclone fence from the fifties still guards the perimeter of the loosely rectangular parcel, and the clothesline runs from one side of the yard to the other like a sad piece of punctuation.

A tiny strip of cracked and weathered concrete circles from the back of the house and meets the front walk.

Humphries turns, giving my mom a condescending smile, and my heart drops. Vincent had offered to buy the place for fifty thousand more.

Plus my body. Might as well sell my soul to the devil.

I swallow, shoring up bravery. "I thought it was worth a bit more."

Mom is silent.

"Yes, well, during the bubble in 2005 to 2007, we could have got mid-threes for this piece. But now"—he shrugs dismissively—"it's only worth what the comps show." He slaps a pile of paperwork on our small kitchen table and gives a grim chin flick toward them. "These are the comparable properties sold in the last three months."

I glance at the papers. My vision blurs as I see figures lower than two hundred thousand. *Damn.*

I look up into his face. He wears a vague and slightly amused smile. I study my Converse shoes, thinking of what to say.

"I could try to put your property on the market for one ninety-nine," he says like he's doing us a favor.

I meet his eyes again. "Thank you for coming, Mr. Humphries," I manage to choke out. "I think my mom and I will need a day to think it over."

"Suit yourself." He reaches out to shake Mom's hand, but she doesn't move.

Shaking hands is painful for her, and he's too stupid to notice her issues.

His lips lift in distaste, and he turns to me. His smile brightens. "I'll leave you with the card of another client of mine who might be willing to pay more before listing."

My heart begins to race. *More? Fantastic.*

He shakes my hand, slipping a business card into my palm. I try not to peek as the pompous prick makes the short way to the door.

I let him out and close the door, carefully engaging the million locks.

Mom's face is sour. "That man is the president of his own fan club."

"Uh-huh," I murmur, opening my hand to check out the card.

Vincent sends his regards, it reads. *Bastard.*

I close my hand in a fist, squeezing my eyes shut. I just gave this loser free reign of my property.

He's obviously the one who set this wheel in motion with the purchase of the commercial buildings that flank our house to the bitter end.

God.

I try not to cry, but the effort makes me want to hyperventilate. Heat suffuses my head, and I sway.

"Shannon, what is it?"

Mom's voice. Worried.

I pry my eyelids open, my arm rigid with holding the damning little note from Vincent the Gangbanger.

"He's not self-important."

"Who?" Mom asks sharply.

"Humphries." I hang my head, and my long hair falls forward. "He's working for Vincent."

I walk to where she sits and hand over the card. Mom carefully unfolds it. "We'll contact another real estate company."

"No," I say. "They're all going to be paid off with this guy's gang money. I bet this entire area of real estate has been tagged for their perusal first."

Mom's face tells me my guess is right.

"I'm going to talk to Vincent."

"Shannon, no—it's not worth your life." With swollen hands Mom tries to grip the edge of her favorite chair, powerless to make me see reason, powerless to make this situation better.

"He's not going to kill me, Mom," I say with a lot more bravado than I feel.

Vincent will just rape me and take my soul. I'll live.

Sort of.

I know where he hangs out.

Smoothing my damp palms over my jeans, I knock on the door of the commercial building that stands to the south of our house. While I wait, my mind wanders to Wring and what he did for me.

Two hoodlums, as Mom would call them, rake their dark eyes up and down my body.

"Hey baby, I got something you need—right here." One grabs his crotch in a gruesome try at a come on.

Why does any man think grabbing his penis is going to be an effective seduction?

I turn away and tense when one of them comes up behind me.

"Hernando was talking to you, crack."

Okay, maybe I was stupid to try to face Vincent head on. I pivot on the top step of the front entrance to the building, and Lead Thug grabs my shoulders, making blowfish kissing noises close to my face.

"Just a taste, *chica*."

"Get your fucking hands off her."

I'm released so fast I stumble, and a hand steadies me.

I twist at my torso and find that hard grip belongs to Vincent.

"Hey, bitch," he says to me in greeting.

"Ah!" the gangbanger behind me says. "*You're* calling her a bitch."

"She's not free game, Hernando. She's *my* bitch."

I clench my teeth. I'll let his dumb comment ride until I can find out what I can get.

Or what I can't.

Standing next to him again, I realize how big he is. I gulp my fear like a bitter pill. His nose is taped, and heavy bruising in half-moon swaths run from the bridge of his nose to nearly his temples, crossing below his evil beady brown eyes.

Wring did this to his face.

A flutter of pure anxiety starts inside my breastbone just thinking about Wring and what his reaction to me being here would be.

It would be bad.

But he's not responsible for me. I'm responsible for myself. And Mom.

I take a deep breath. Resolution kicks my ass, and sheer stupidity propels me forward. "We need to talk."

His hands run down my arms, and I shiver in revulsion, but Vincent smiles. "I knew you'd see things my way, baby."

I'll never see things his way.

He pulls me by my hand inside the building, and a bunch of gang members look up from their various pursuits.

A man is between a woman's legs and she's groaning, shoving her hips into his face. I quickly look away, only to be visually assaulted by a man's naked hips piston humping another woman from behind.

My stomach rolls, and I try looking straight ahead.

But I'm not blind to my periphery, where another guy snorts drugs through his nose, using a dirty glass table top as a platform.

Someone who is even bigger than Vincent walks toward us with purpose in his stride.

Oh God.

"This the bitch that you've got a boner for?" His lips twist.

"Yeah," Vincent replies.

Eyes bright with anger, the guy nods.

Then he backhands me.

I spin, landing on my knees, using my good hand to avoid falling flat on my face. Blood drops splatter across the rough cement floor, and I cry out, my cheek instantly aflame.

Not sure what I expected, but getting beat up wasn't really it.

"Don't, *jefe*. I'll keep the bitch in line."

Surprise, surprise, Vincent wants to beat me, but nobody else can.

"Nope," he snarls, "she brought those fucking Road Kill bastards in to protect her."

I didn't. But that doesn't matter, because this guy believes I did.

He yanks me up by the back of my pants, and I don't even think about how strong a man would have to be to do that to a full-grown woman.

Rolling nausea churns in my stomach. "Please!" I throw up my arm in front of my face, and he tears it away, eyes blazing into mine.

We look each other over.

A smile starts to break over his face, and I'm surprised to notice how handsome he would be if he weren't Vincent's leader. If his hair weren't so greasy.

If he hadn't belted me.

"I like her, Vincent." He thrashes me. Hard. My head leaps back and forward. "You that fucker's property?"

What?

I shake my head, saying no without words seems safest.

"No MC fuck is going to come between a Blood and pussy unless he's got a stake in shit."

More shaking. My teeth click together, and I reactively grab his leather coat to stop the horrible jarring.

He smirks.

"I don't know what you mean about property," I say quietly, licking blood off my lip and trying to sound calm. Reasonable.

He turns to Vincent, who seems to do everything but tuck his tail between his legs. "Is she fucking retarded?"

Vincent shakes his head. "No, hoss. She's pure. Innocent."

His face whips to mine. "You got a cherry, bitch?"

The crowd of gang members around us grows.

Oh God. Oh God. Oh God.

Hymen?

I don't know how to respond. If I say yes—will they *not* do the unthinkable? If I say no, will they gang rape me? My expression must be all dumb.

He slaps me again.

I go down again, hard.

118

"Stop hitting me," I growl from all fours on the ground.

"Then fucking *speak*, bitch."

I don't cry. I stand.

"I'm Shannon Berg. I'm trying to make a deal."

The *jefe* watches me. I know from my Spanish in high school the name means "boss."

He waves a palm, telling me to go on.

The crowd of gangbangers is silent. A dozen eyes that mean me harm watch my every movement.

"Vincent said he'd pay me two hundred fifty thousand for our house." I point to the north, wincing as my tongue runs along my cut lip.

The boss throws his head back, giving a belly laugh. "Yup. That's right, little cherry. Two hundred K for the hood, and fifty K for you."

My heart thumps. "What?" I whisper.

"For your hymen, Shannon," he says, pronouncing my name like he's still saying *bitch*. "Your white little perfection. Lots of men will pay top dollar for an intact snatch."

I retreat a step as though slapped. "And if I'm not?"

He takes back the step I gained and looms over me. His breath is rank, his gaze is predatory. "Then we all get a taste of you—now."

The group tightens around us, and one grabs my breast. I yelp, though it didn't hurt.

"No!" Vincent roars. "I wanted her. She's mine!"

The boss chuckles, extracting a gun from the small of his back, and presses the barrel to Vincent's forehead.

The blast is deafening.

Men duck, hitting the floor.

Blood slaps my face like a spray of heated rain. A tiny warm something tumbles down the front of my face. It makes a splat sound when it lands.

Realizing my eyes are closed, I open them.

Bits of skull have pierced my skin. I see them like cream shadows underneath my eyes. I hear a sound like mewling then recognize it as my own voice.

As I turn away from Vincent's blown-away head, heat drives up from my toenails. I open my mouth to breathe, but it fills with the taste of metal, and I throw up on top of one of the gangbangers.

"Bitch!" He rolls away and stands, hands fisted.

Fingers grab the back of my shirt and hauls me backward. Another hand pile drives into my hair, cranking my head back.

The taste of raw bile chokes me. and I cough as I gaze into the eyes of a man far worse than Vincent.

"You a virgin?" he screams in my face, and the fine hairs that have come loose from my ponytail lift with the scourge of his breath. "Because one of my dogs just bit the hand that feeds him. Nobody tells me what's theirs. What's theirs is *mine*."

His face hovers above me, wearing a matching mask of gore.

"Well?" he bellows.

I nod.

His smile becomes a grin. "Good." He shoves me away, and I slip on the stuff on the floor.

The stuff that used to be Vincent.

11

WRING

Sweat runs through my shorn hair, splattering on my trembling shoulders.

"Two-forty," Noose says.

I don't completely stiffen my elbows.

Noose cups his hands around the barbell in case I drop the weights. Never have.

He still spots me anyway, so I don't go *splat*.

Our eyes meet. "One more rep, pussy." His smile is crooked but guarded. It's a lot of weight to push.

I've let myself get bulky since I separated from the Navy. Then, I couldn't afford to be. Needed to be fast, lithe. Now I'm letting nature take its course. I want to be strong and use the strength to defend.

We'll always have stealth.

I control my breathing, centering everything I have, everything I am on the lift.

I let it down without a clink.

Noose lifts his eyebrows in direct challenge, the prick.

I scowl.

"Whatever it takes," he hikes a shoulder.

I let the breath ease out of me. My thoughts are a pinpoint. I lift, huffing out a couple of sharp breathes. Get to the end.

"One, two, three," Noose says quietly.

I let the weight down slowly.

No clanking.

"Goddamn. Rock solid." Noose holds his fist up, and I tap it between blowing out oxygen.

Spent as fuck.

"You can still do more," I mention.

"Fuck it. Got an inch on ya and twenty pounds."

Noose isn't a cut guy, more Spartan.

I'm a little more cut, leaner. But bench pressing two-forty thirty times isn't bad. I would love to do Noose's two-sixty.

We walk over to an empty weight bench, and I sit on a stool across from it. We lift our bottled waters at the same time.

"I'd give my left nut for a beer. Fuck water," Noose comments dryly.

I raise the water bottle. "Beer doesn't hydrate."

"Like I give a fuck?"

I grin. "Probably not."

"We doing flutters today?" I ask, because it's easier to concentrate on working my body rather than getting to what I'm really wanting to know. It's only been one day since Viper called emergency church and didn't beat me down too bad.

He didn't give a green light, either.

We upend the waters and crush the empties, tossing them in the trash for Storm to clean up later.

"Nah. Don't feel like being on my back and abusing the abs." He leans forward and punches me in the gut. But I hardened up in anticipation.

"You don't feel like you need flutters." He gives me a look, swinging his fingers out, cracking up. Fucker loves pain.

I shake my head, stifling a grin at his abused hand. "Just wanted to do a thousand and hand you your ass."

He gives me a sideways look of disbelief. "A thousand?"

I nod.

"Impressive."

I shrug. "The core's everything, brother."

"God, don't start singing the mantra from BUDS."

I smirk, and we sit in companionable silence for a few extended heartbeats.

Finally, Noose says, "She's a librarian." He shrugs.

He got right on shit. Another reason to like Noose. He's a man of his word.

"I know that. That tidbit's about as worthless as tits on a nun."

Noose laughs, holding his ribs. "Nice."

I fold my arms, cupping my elbows. Everything hurts after lifting. Joints. Muscles. Mind. Trying to keep my thoughts off Shannon has become a part-time job.

Not fucking working.

And, I thought I was sleeping bad before? Don't know why I bother going to bed at all.

"Does she have any hidden kids or anything?"

Noose scowls. "No. Not that there's anything wrong with kids."

I grunt. "They shit, eat, and wail. Not always in that order."

Noose appears to contemplate my comment then laughs. "Yeah."

I swing my palm out. "Tell me the rest."

He looks between his hands, his finger running down a printout. "Shannon Berg." He looks up at me suddenly. "I feel like a stalker."

"Whatever the fuck. Spill your guts."

"Fine, ya foul fucker." He exhales, flexing his calloused hand. "Almost twenty-five. You know her physical stats."

His eyes squint at me, glinting with humor. "Family's had the little house since 1910, one of the first families in the valley."

"Not much left," I comment mostly to myself.

"Wouldn't be. Dad was killed in a farm accident working his family's land when she was a baby. Mom's got some disease. Anyway, scabbed the medical records for the mom—doesn't have long."

Ah.

"My guess is Shannon is taking care of her mom, trying to work a job close to her house. Vincent sees her coming and going, takes note of that prime little chunk of real estate, and wants it. Figures he can put the screws to Shannon and get it for less than market."

"So she's desperate to stay," I guess slowly. Her behavior makes sense with the facts Noose is telling me.

"Sounds right. But"—Noose ducks his head—"you're not going to like this."

I grin, baring my teeth like a pleased shark. "Lay it on me."

"Uh-huh. Well, I got Shannon's medical records, too."

"How did you manage that?"

Noose's dirty-blond eyebrows hike. "Please. I'm a hacking fool."

I chuckle. "*Right.* Okay, go on." I wave my palm impatiently, dabbing at the sweat from my workout with a hand towel.

Noose shifts his weight on the bench.

"Spit it the fuck out. What does she have? HIV or something?"

He shakes his head, light steel-colored eyes meeting mine. "Worse."

What? I scrunch my face. Pressing my fists against my knees, I lean forward on the stool.

"Virgin." The word drops out of his mouth like a bomb.

I abruptly stand, giving him the disbelief he deserves like a gunshot between the eyes. "No girl is a virgin at twenty-four."

Noose chuckles. "You got a point, brother. Pretty rare. But I'm thinking this is one reason Vincent might want her."

I hang my head. I have to want a chick that's a virgin. That the Bloods want to sell to the highest bidder. Who's some kind of a Mother Teresa and stays home to take care of her dying mother.

Of all the complicated fucking women I can go after…

Noose rolls his shoulders into a shrug. "If *I* can find out this personal stuff about her"—he stabs his chest with his thumb—"so can the Bloods. It makes sense they'd look into her." His eyes are steady on mine. "They want Shannon's property so they can have a whole block of gang bullshit. Then one of them notices Shannon…" His voice dips into a valley. His exhale is tired, and for the first time, I notice the dark circles under his eyes.

Fuck. What he's saying makes perfect sense, but I don't have to like it.

I get out of my head long enough to ask, "Thought you were sleeping okay?"

He snorts, lighting up a cig, then puffs a ring into the humid gym air. "Aria wakes up all night to eat."

I give an almost imperceptible shudder.

"Bum a smoke?"

"Sure," Noose hits the top of the box, and a cig pops partway out.

I grab it.

"I'll help you put another nail in your coffin." He winks. "Love smoking in the workout room."

He blows two rings. The smaller fitting within the larger.

I laugh.

"Vipe would have a shit fit if he saw us dirtying up the exercise room."

Noose chuckles. "Yeah."

We smoke, and I think about Vincent lying in wait for a vulnerable woman who doesn't have a shred of hope and has never been with a man.

Purity like that doesn't have a place in this world. And I had her up against a wall, dry humping her. A pang of guilt hits me hard. Shannon deserves better than me.

After a couple of minutes, I repeat in quiet awe, "Virgin."

"Yup. Know for a fact. Got codes for that shit. Got a code if a chick's ever had an abortion, too. Med codes. Know 'em all."

I screw my face up into a frown. "That's fucked up."

Noose stabs his cig out on the sole of his boot. "Yeah."

No one's ever accused us of being normal.

"I don't like you knowing Shannon's a virgin."

Noose barks out a laugh, starts coughing, and howls.

I glare at him.

"I don't give two fucks. I got Rose. These are the facts. Nobody's had that pussy, and the Bloods are think-ing she's a hot commodity. They kill two birds with one stone. Get the chick's property that they need. Get a bunch of money for her. Maybe kill the mom, make it look like the old ticker gave out or some other bit of fuckery."

"They're not getting Shannon."

"Listen, Wring—"

"Don't."

"Let this go. I know that you feel bad for the girl, but she's probably not worth it—all things considered."

His unspoken words are: Club first. Chicks second.

My chin hikes, and I look him square in the eye. "What if she is?"

Seconds pound by, turning into a full minute.

"Fuck," Noose mutters, then after a protracted moment, he grins. "Let's knot up."

I nod. *Reconnaissance is in order.*

Noose grabs my arm as we leave the club. "We don't do anything unless they're killing her."

A hot minute of indecision grips us.

"I'm not letting them rape or beat her up, brother."

Noose grimaces. "Fuck no, I gotcha."

"We take Lariat," I say.

He pulls a face.

"You gotta get over this bullshit from our tour."

He walks off. "When the time's right."

We stride to our rides. "When will you know?" I ask to his broad back. I hate the bad blood between him and Lariat. They've got to settle that shit. Not good for the club. Hell, it's not good for them.

"I'll know."

He hops on his Road King and slams another cig between his lips, cups the flame, and shoots out a ring. As he turns on the motor, I text Lariat the deets.

He texts back*:*

Affirmative.

Turning my face to the horizon, I pocket my cell. The color of sunset spills tangerine and pink light across the treetops that surround the club, making spatter patterns on the old bunker like battered fruit.

"Lariat on board?" Noose asks over the loud vibration of his engine.

I nod.

We were a team once. Noose and Lariat might have unresolved issues, but we'll always be a team.

SEALs in the service, SEALs for life.

Noose swings his head in the direction of Shannon's house as we cruise past.

And we keep cruising past the newer industrial buildings that flank it. Memories of pinning her against the wall right outside her front door give me get a hard-on at the worst time.

We go almost to Noose's place and glide into two parking spots.

Noose and I kill the engines then step off our rides simultaneously.

We don't speak.

Lariat walks to our position.

"Where's your ride?" Noose asks.

"Your condo."

Noose scowls. "Don't want to lead those fuckers back to my family."

"Not gonna happen, Noose." Lariat scowls. "Rose will chop their nuts off if they get within spitting distance."

"Don't want her to have to, numb nuts."

They face off.

I snap my fingers. "Wake up, fuckers. Shannon. We're here to talk to her, see if we can help."

They glare at each other.

We take off our leather jackets, fold them, and place them in our trunks at the back of our bikes.

Lariat moves across the street, walking parallel to me and Noose.

We go to her house, where a single light is burning behind a curtain.

I knock, and Lariat stands across the street, looking conspicuous as fuck.

A voice from behind the door calls out, "Who is it?"

Fuck. Not Shannon.

Noose mouths, "Mom."

"Sam Walker, ma'am."

Noose claps a hand over his mouth. I elbow him in his side.

Some locks twist, and a chain is the only thing standing between Shannon's mom and me.

"Are you the bike rider?" she asks, a pale-blue eyeball peering between the two-inch space.

Shannon mentioned me? Good or bad, I think for a heartbeat.

Her eye shifts to Noose. He flutters his fingers. "Hello, ma'am."

Her lips thin.

Damn.

Here goes. "Yes."

She seems relieved. "A pleasure to make your acquaintance."

My shoulders drop, body singing with a tension I didn't even know I had.

I nod. "Same here."

She frowns. "Is Shannon with you?"

Her mom tries to look around me, and I tense.

Noose and I exchange a glance. He'd already mentioned she was off work.

"No."

Her eyes go wide. "She…I—" Tears form.

"Mrs. Berg," I say in a neutral, calming way, "where is Shannon?"

"She was supposed to be home a half hour ago."

Not good.

"You stay here. If we're not back in a half hour, call 9-1-1."

"I don't know you," she states the obvious, and my fingers curl around the partly open door.

I could force it open, but I only nod. "Yeah. But I'm protecting Shannon."

"Why?" Her voice quivers.

I'm honest. Like usual. "I don't know."

Noose put his face beside mine. "Sorry ma'am, that'll have to be good enough."

He pulls me away, and we jog out of there. Toward the nearest building.

Toward Shannon.

12

SHANNON

My knees immediately soak with blood, and I shriek, leaping up and stumbling away.

Hands grab me and keep me from falling again.

The boss walks toward me.

I can't stop screaming. Blood and bits of human brain and skull stick to his face, throat, and clothes like measles of death.

He blinks, and his eyes appear stranded within all the blood droplets.

I gag.

His hands land on my shoulders, and I smell gun powder.

"Listen, and listen close. You're mine now. I want that fucking house you got, and I want what I can get outta you. Got it?"

I don't nod. I don't move.

"Nod your head that you understand. Because permission's not a part of this."

"My mom," I gasp.

"Your fucking breath reeks." He grins.

Of course it does. I just puked.

"What about your mom? Who gives a fuck? We'll do the old bitch—hell, it's a mercy. Hear she's sicker than a dog." His grin spreads wider, and he gives a manic snicker.

I close my eyes.

When I open them, he's still there—in front of me like a demonic apparition.

The rumble of bikes mixes with the white noise of the gangbangers' activities.

Oh *no.*

"Thought you said that fucker Wring wasn't your man."

I shake my head. "He's not." I'm not involving Wring in this. It's my mess. But fear saturates my insides.

"I'd know the sound of those Road Kill MC fuckers anywhere."

A full minute passes, the gangbangers quiet like church mice. Listening.

A deliberate pounding on the door startles everyone. A dozen sets of eyes flow to the door.

"Fuck." The boss's eyes move over my face, filled with acute irritation and disdain.

"Clean this mess up," he says, and three gang members trot over to Vincent's body.

Oh God. I swallow more vomit.

"Not your man, eh?" He shakes me by my arm, jarring my wrist, and I yelp.

"Vince fuck up your hand? Gonna stop you from giving blow jobs, sweet thing?" His tongue lashes the top of my ear, and I cringe.

His face swings to the loose circle of gang members, who step away from the steel door. "Wait by the door."

"Who's there?" he asks and pinches my butt cheek, and I muffle a cry of pain. The boss claps a hand over my mouth, fingers biting along my face, numbing it.

"Road Kill MC," a deep voice says from the other side.

The boss's smile comes online like a piranha's grin. "Open the door."

Two gangbangers open the door, knives in their hands.

Please don't hurt Wring, I have time to think.

The boss puts me in front of him like a shield.

The door swings open, and there stands Wring, the last of the western sunlight backlighting him.

His face is in shadow, but I see enough of his expression to interpret his feelings.

I see murder on his face. Theirs.

My fist comes down once, twice, three times.

Third time's the charm. I drop a bleeding gangbanger on the steps in front of the building, and he cooperatively drapes over the cement treads like a human rug. Just out of our path.

Noose steps away from the other two. They're out cold.

"We're fucked now," Noose says in a conversational tone.

I put my hands on my hips. "If they'd just been open to some honest-to-God discourse."

Noose quirks a brow, cracking his raw knuckles. "Right." He tries to eyeball his front. "Got any blood on my cut?"

My eyes sweep down his cut. I hold my thumb and index almost together.

Noose grunts. "God*dammit.* Dry cleaning bills get excessive. Should have left it in the trunk with the leather."

I don't point out that if we weren't beating people up regularly, it wouldn't be an issue.

Lariat smirks.

He pounds on the steel door, and a full reverberating echo sounds, making the interior of the building ring empty.

We know it's not.

I hear shuffling of feet, and our knots come out.

The first thing I see is Shannon. Can't say I was anticipating her being right there.

Navy SEALs are trained in basic EMT skills, and I'm handy enough to know when I see the beginnings of shock.

Shannon's got them. Her skin's gray, and she's wearing brains and blood. Back spray from a close-range shot.

The Blood who's got his hands on her is going to die. He holds her like he owns her.

That's the moment when I know I've been kidding myself.

Shannon's mine.

"Luis Lopez," I say with a calm I don't feel.

"Road Kill scum," he acknowledges.

"We were gonna be all polite and shit, but now I don't feel compelled," Noose says.

"We came to get the girl," I say, not looking away from Lopez. I know he's king.

And the king of the Bloods has my girl.

A girl I haven't claimed.

My eyes flick to hers. Shannon blinks, licks her lip, and grimaces at the taste of someone else's blood. Her gaze also pleads for me to let her go.

Fuck that.

"She your property?" Lopez licks the top of her ear, and she cringes away from him.

The fibers of my rope feel like individual threads of death in my hand. Lopez's death.

My tongue runs over my lip, anticipating a rope on a certain throat. "Yeah." A weight I didn't know I was carrying lifts. Sometimes it just feels straight up good to admit shit.

Shannon quickly shakes her head.

"Shut up, bitch!" he growls, and his lips close around the top of her ear.

Tears streak down her face, making clear paths through the drying blood.

Lopez's eyes go to my knot, which is subtly turned to do damage. He snorts, yanking Shannon. Her injured arm bangs against his hip, and she yelps.

"You think your little rope's gonna do anything?"

Noose and Lariat are as silent as the grave.

Lopez swivels his chin to the sides of us, and his minions come at us with knives. Shannon gives a big tell, tensing to her left.

I whip out the double knot and take the knife from dickless at my left, hitting the hilt hard.

The knife skitters, and I snap the weighted end, where one knot is larger than the other, hitting him in the nose.

Cartilage explodes, sending a geyser of blood out of each nostril.

"Get them," Lopez bellows.

"Let go!" Shannon screams. Her heels make marks in the blood as he drags her from the fighting.

Four more men come at us, and I wonder where the guns are.

Shannon collapses, and Lopez doesn't anticipate the move.

I love her for it.

I toss the knot I used on dickless at Lopez.

Like a bola, it swings, hitting him in his arrogant snout. He bleats like a wounded goat, hands coming to his face.

Shannon crawls toward me.

I can't deal with saving her right then because two guys land on me.

I wrap the rope hard on the neck biter who tries to latch on to me through my cut.

Gotta love leather.

He flies over my back and onto the floor, effectively hanging himself on my shorty length.

Squeezing, I uncross my arms, and he flops to the floor like a rag doll.

"Wring!" Shannon screams.

And our eyes lock.

I see her warning and duck, swiping a longer length out, and use it like a tripping wire.

Two guys tumble past me like bowling pins.

Noose roars, and I spare a glance.

He's got three down. All unconscious.

Lariat's got the door.

Only Lopez is left.

He's got a gun. He points it at me.

I see my death. I've seen it a lot in my life.

A slender leg swings, hitting the gun as it fires. The bullet goes wide, embedding in the unfinished insulated ceiling.

Fiberglass rains down like spun sugar. I run to Shannon and scoop her up.

"Fuckers!" Lopez yells.

Noose kicks the smoking gun away from Lopez, and it skitters across the concrete like an out-of-control metal insect.

We leave him alive as a sign of goodwill. The others lay beat up and bleeding, but alive.

I cradle Shannon against me, and Noose takes rear position, securing my back, as Lariat leads.

We leave as we came. In violence.

"Mom can't see me like this," I say as soon as we get back to where the guys' bikes sit.

"No shit?" Noose says with a snort.

"Come on, have a little compassion," Wring says.

Noose laughs silently. "Feeling great," he says.

Wring's eyes move heavenward. "Because we used knots?"

He nods, throws a fist in the air, and they bump fists.

"I'll take Shannon to Vipe's place in Ravensdale, get this shit figured out and clean her up."

I hear the other biker guy fire up his bike and watch him for a second or two as he pulls out.

He gives Wring and Noose a nod and leaves.

Noose turns his attention back to me. "I can have Storm drop by your place and," he throws a hand up, "tell your mom shit's okay."

"Please put me down," I say to Wring.

He does, and I grip his arm to keep standing. "They might retaliate—hurt Mom." I can't stand the thought of that.

"Nah." Noose winds his long hair at his nape and reties it, man-bun style. "Fucking Bloods don't have the cojones." He grabs a pack of cigarettes out of a pouch between his handlebars, puts one between his lips, and lights up in a sequence of moves so smooth they look orchestrated. A ring plumes out of his mouth.

I watch it float into a sky filling with glittering stars, and out of nowhere, I start shaking.

His eyes narrow on me. "Shock," Noose states.

My teeth start to chatter.

"Yeah, fuck," Wring agrees, and I try to sit down on the curb.

"Nope, can't stick around." His face whips to Noose's, and I watch and listen to the interaction like I'm having an out-of-body experience. "Text Storm, get his ass over here on the QT."

"On it," Noose says, extracting a cell and punching in stuff.

Wring turns my face with gentle fingers. "Listen, Shannon."

I nod.

"Taking you somewhere safe, quiet."

Quiet's good.

"You can't faint."

No fainting. I start to laugh.

"Hey," he says softly, "don't freak out right now. I need you to wait until I can transport you."

Wring settles me on the curb and puts a tender hand on my neck, pushing my head between my knees. "Breathe, babe."

I breathe and concentrate only on that.

Not on the fact that Luis Lopez has marked me. Or that Mom's in danger.

Or that I'm going off with Wring from a motorcycle gang.

Covered in Vincent's brains.

I just breathe.

13

My fingers are numb by the time we get to this place Wring told me about in Ravensdale.

Thank God he lent me his leather jacket. I've never seen him wear it, only the leather vest with the patches on it. There's a Road Kill MC patch and a little red, diamond-shaped one with the one-percenter symbol. *Whatever that means.*

I pray that somehow that other guy, Storm, will get to my house and calm Mom down. But these biker guys are rough, so Mom feeling calm may not happen.

I sigh against his back.

Wring pulls up in a semi-circular gravel drive and parks in front of deep and wide wood steps.

Night has come, and I can't make out much. But the structure looks like a smallish log cabin sitting perfectly on a small knoll. Graceful branches from well-established cedar trees sweep the corners of the roof like sentinels.

Wring shuts off the bike and holds out his arm. I take it gratefully and slide off.

My teeth are back to chattering.

Wring gets off and takes my hand, tugging me behind him as he taps a quick text to someone. I stumble up the stairs, and with a soft curse, he shoves his cell in his pocket and dips to literally sweep me off my feet.

"Sorry," I mutter, exhausted.

He gets to the front door and plucks a key that dangles from the same chain as his wallet and inserts it into a keyhole.

With a low shriek, the door opens wide.

A dim interior forges shapes of growing shadows as the deepening of the night seeps from the edges toward where we stand.

"Gotta get you a shower." He kicks the door shut behind us, and a latch falls into place.

I want a shower worse than I've ever wanted anything in my life.

"Wring," I call softly.

He ignores me, moving into a tiny bathroom with barely enough room to fit a person inside. A toilet stands crammed between the shower stall and a minuscule sink and vanity combination.

"Yeah?" he asks, holding me against him with one hand and turning on the shower with the other.

"I can—I'll clean up."

Wring studies me, shadows fleeing when he snaps on a light. The naked bulb blares down at us.

"I know that. But we're hooking up. Tonight."

"What?" I ask, and my hands go to his massive shoulders. If I tried, I could probably tuck my head underneath his chin; he's that big.

"Hooking up?" My voice sounds like a squeak.

"I'm cleaning this shit off you, and then I'm fucking you, Shannon. You're going to be my property."

I shake my head, denying him, though his words make my lady parts throb. My face infuses with heat—I remember what he did to me against that wall. I'll never forget. But him *telling* me what to do?

No.

That's what that Blood did. Luis Lopez hit me, then he killed Vincent.

Wring caresses my face, and I pull away. "I'm dirty." Fresh tears brim over my eyes and sink into the old tracks of the last ones. "I have to get...I have to get clean." I don't want Wring to touch any part of me while I'm covered with someone's liquefied body.

"I know. You've been through a lot, and I shouldn't lay this on you."

My gaze locks with his. "But you will."

Wring pushes me up against the wall, narrowly missing a towel ring. "Yeah. I will. You put yourself in harm's way, Shannon. What in the righteous fuck did you think you were doing going over to Blood territory?"

Steam from the shower rises.

I don't answer. I can't think of a response that makes any sense.

"Ya know what? Fuck it."

Wring pins my wrists above my head and tears my filthy shirt over my head, pulling my wrists away from the wall. Then he tosses the shirt outside the bathroom.

Vincent's blood didn't soak through to the skin, and my boobs bounce in time with my heaving chest.

Wring's eyes latch on to my chest. "Fuck, you're a gorgeous girl."

He dips his head and, still holding my wrists, dives his face between my breasts, kissing the flesh there. My emotions are so raw—so close to the surface—I go from angry to lustful instantly. Still holding my wrists, he uses his other hand to scoop my boob out of my lacy bra. He takes my nipple into my mouth.

Each erotic pull is a tender thread that tweaks deep at my core, and I moan at the new sensation.

"Yeah, baby," Wring murmurs and drops my wrist to tug my bra off. He doesn't bother with finesse, just grips the straps and yanks. It slides down one of my arms, and I fling it off.

Next, he unhooks the waistband of my jeans and slides them over my hips.

His hand cups my sex over my sheer panties, and I catch my breath. Can't take another breath.

Or think.

"Gotta get you clean, Shannon."

I nod and manage to gasp a *yes* in there somewhere.

Wring's angry that I went over to the Bloods' territory and tried to reason with Vincent.

But none of that matters when his hands are on my body.

Suddenly, I'm naked, and I'm sure Wring will ravage me. Instead, he gently places me underneath the running water. I'm drenched in seconds.

Soap runs over my body as his hands clean me. He swipes away the remnants of Vincent off my face, and suds run pink with what's left. I shut my eyes tight.

Shampoo and firm hands lather my hair, and I sigh, letting water run inside my mouth and drip off my chin. His sure hands glide down my sides, framing my ribs, his thumbs a breath away from my breasts.

"Shannon," Wring says softly, and I open my eyes.

"I'm no rapist."

I give a languid smile. His hands warm me, soothe me, and clean me. "No," I readily agree.

"I want to come in there with you."

The expression in his eyes is almost painful. He's waiting for me to reject him. If I was even a little bit smart, I would.

I'm not.

"Yes."

Wring strips out of his clothes in record time and stands there, letting me look at him.

He spreads his powerful arms away from his body, a faint smile hovering at his full lips. "Like what you see?"

I nod, putting my face in my hands, and cry. I'm so thankful he saved me from that horrible guy.

"Hey, shhh…" He bends down to take my hands away then kisses my face.

"Thank you, Wring."

"Oh, baby—I tried to fight it. Can't. Gotta have you. The moment you put those green eyes on me, I couldn't get away, say *no*. Nothing. But hear me." He tips my face up, and I meet his nearly translucent eyes, the color of glaciers tinged by blue. "Don't have sex with me—or do anything with me—'cause of gratitude. I'm not going to be a mercy fuck, baby."

I start giggling.

He frowns. I pull him into the shower, and our bodies touch, my bare breasts mashing against his ribcage.

Wring puts a hand beside my face, and the molded plastic shower back is cold against my skin. I wince.

He pulls me tight against him and I feel his erection.

Scary.

Exciting.

"You laughing at me?" His lips twist into a smile. Wring takes ahold of my wet hair and flings it behind my back.

"No," I say, cradling his face. "You—I don't think anyone would have sex with you out of mercy, Wring. You're safe there." I give him a speculative look. "Maybe they'd beg for mercy."

His hands run down my sides, tickling me, and I squeal. The laughter feels so good, I hiccup back more.

Wring's hands go to my breasts, mounding them, and my laughter fades. "Beg," he whispers beside my temple, and I shiver against him.

My breath stills as water runs over his shoulders and between his hands, settling and filling between my breasts. He kisses first one nipple then moves to the next.

My hand sinks over his skull. The short hairs stand stiff and wet underneath my hand.

"Gonna clean ya," he whispers against my skin.

I nod, realize he can't see me, and say, "Yes."

His hands find my wetness easily, and I move my knees apart.

"Shannon," he breathes against me, and before I know it, his dexterous fingers have split my folds. I throw my head back, wrapping my arms around his neck.

His fingers leave me, and I groan at their absence. But Wring's not through with me yet. He hikes me up and puts his face against my sex.

His breath is hot.

I automatically tense, stopping him with a hand, though I know if he wanted to keep going, nothing could stop him.

No man goes to these lengths to rape me after he's saved me twice.

My inexperience makes me unsure, though.

"What?" he asks, eyes rolling up from between my legs to fasten on my face.

I swallow, embarrassed. "I've never done this."

Wring grins, and his cheek moves against my inner thigh, rubbing it like a cat. "That's okay."

Then his mouth is on my center, and I yell out.

I feel him smile against my slickness, then his tongue is working my clit, while the fingers of one hand play against my entrance.

Back and forth, his mouth presses against me.

"Wring," I struggle, pleasant heat suffusing my vagina.

"Hang tight. Gonna make you blow."

Blow? Oh yeah—cum.

I close my eyes, momentarily relaxing, and one more swirl with his tongue at the same time his finger enters me partway. I shudder, my walls pulsing around him, as I push myself against his mouth.

"That's it. Let it go, Shannon."

I do. Everything that's built up inside me rushes out in blissful waves of pleasure.

Wring's fingers bite into the flesh of my butt cheeks while his face is buried in my most sensitive area, and a new wave of pounding pleasure sears through me again.

Gradually, his tongue slows, and he withdraws his finger. He lets me down like I'm made of glass, and I lean against the shower wall in a semi-daze.

"That's the look I like." His smile is proud, satisfied, and content.

"Get me out of here," I say feeling suddenly too hot.

Wring picks me up, sets me on my feet on top of a bath mat, and wraps me carefully inside a huge bath towel. He shakes his head, and tiny droplets of warm water strike my face.

He kisses them.

Wring shuts off the water and binds a towel around his waist. He waggles his eyebrows, and I smile.

Wrapping a strong arm around me, he walks us to a door that is partially ajar. "Do you proper here," he says.

He sets me on the bed, and the towel falls away from my breasts.

Wring stares at the view just as a stray beam of moonlight hits my body. "You make me crazy, Shannon."

He makes me crazy, too.

My inhale is sharp. Reluctant. "I have to tell you something, Wring. It's important."

He's probably been with a hundred women. And I've never been with a man.

Not once.

He strides to me, whipping the towel off his waist and tossing it on the back of a chair.

Naked, he sinks to his haunches and pushes my legs wide. Only my bunched damp towel is between us.

My eyes latch onto his penis. I gulp at the size.

I tremble. "I'm a virgin." I clench my fingers tightly, feeling stupid.

Feeling brave.

When I look up at Wring, his eyes are solemn. Then a grin breaks out, moonlight caressing his expression.

"That's okay," he says a second time.

I smile.

14

Wring doesn't attack the obvious. He moves slowly as I lie back on the soft unmade bed.

First, his lips touch the bone at the inside of my ankle, his left hand moving slowly up my calf, kneading the flesh.

"I can't believe—"

"Shhh, Shannon, believe me when I say I'm not going anywhere."

I hike up on my elbows, and his face is between my thighs. Again.

"What's 'property'?"

His expression arranges into tight lines of irritation. "It's a MC term. Means you belong only to me."

Wring's strong hands press my thighs apart.

I want this, but I'm afraid of what giving that piece of me up means. Afraid to enter into a culture I know nothing about. Afraid for my future. Tomorrow—and beyond.

Then Wring's thumb sweeps across my open entrance, spread as wide as a woman can be and still have legs, and my breath stills in my throat. Caught. Hot. Wanting.

His teeth lightly abrade my labia, and I shudder, my hands finding his head.

"You like it," he says, and his voice vibrates against my sensitive flesh.

Oh God. "Yes."

Wring made me cum in the shower, and he'll make me get close now.

"I don't have a hymen—lost it when I was riding horses at my grandfather's ranch."

He lifts his head, an amused smile ghosting his lips. "Why did you wait?" he asks after a heartbeat.

I don't know. I could use Mom as an excuse—and that's the truth. The real truth hurts too much. That I let taking care of someone else get in the way of taking care of myself. I've never allowed myself to live.

Mom's right. Her affliction has stolen my life's time.

And I'm here to take it back. Right now, with this man. This moment. But what I say aloud is, "I just never found the right man." And that's true, too.

Wring accepts what I say at face value as his tongue finds me again, and I writhe under the hot wet touch he provides.

Crawling up my body, he leaves my drenched entrance and works up to my face, trailing kisses. Cradling my face in his hands, he looks deeply into my eyes as his cock moves into position between my legs.

"You don't have to. But whether or not we do this now or later, you're mine."

I knew I was his when he beat down Vincent, then when he came for me at the gangbanger's place. I just couldn't let myself believe that a turn of fate would shape itself into this moment with Wring.

I can't deny it. "I know."

His eyes are serious, never leaving mine. "I won't lie—this is gonna hurt. Even though I made you ready, it'll hurt."

I nod. I definitely know the mechanics. I've isolated myself by choice, but I understood what to do.

And if the shower is a taste of what sex with Wring is, I'm so ready to be with him. Still, I'm tense as Wring begins to rock inside my body. The first bit of him inside me feels incredible, stretching and filling me perfectly.

As he goes deeper, my body resists. Never having had a penis inside keeps me from relaxing. My walls clench around the foreign invader, and I still. Trying to stave off the image of how all that size is inside me.

"No," he holds my head, forcing me to see only him. "Look at me while I'm in you, Shannon."

My eyes find his, and he presses in another burning inch. "Hurts," I whisper.

Wring nods, and a slight smile take hold of his lips. "Hot as fuck that I'm the only prick that's ever been in your pussy."

A short laugh bursts from between my lips, and my muscles spasm around him. We groan together.

"You have a way with words," I breathe through my pain.

Wring places his forehead against mine. "I say what I'm thinking. I know it's not smooth. It's crude. But it's me, Shannon—and you're getting all of me. No one else. Just you."

He pushes stray hairs out of my face and kisses me.

I lift my hips, and he slides in the rest of the way. I gasp at the feeling of fullness, and Wring throbs inside me.

"It's so hard not to go inside you, baby. You're so tight. Fucking perfection."

"Why don't you?" I swivel my hips a little, and my pussy gives an answering pulse to the motion. I groan at the sensation.

As the initial pain recedes, Wring feels so good.

He chuckles. "Because I want you to come around my cock."

Sliding a hand between our bodies, he begins to swirl my moist clit, and I sigh, my thighs automatically falling farther apart. Then Wring begins to move deeply inside once more.

"Ah," he breathes and rises up on his hands, push-up style, pressing deep and withdrawing, thrusting in slow rhythmic pushes of flesh.

I meet each one, burning beginning to give way to pleasure.

Wring sits on his knees and grabs my hips, bringing my body back and forth, using it to fuck him. The sight of his length buried inside me causes my pussy to squeeze and release around him.

"Stop," Wring says through clenched teeth. "I'm gonna go."

I *can't* stop. His thumb has found my clit again and works it hard, swirling and rubbing, peeling back the small hood and flicking a fingernail over the sensitive tip.

He seats himself with a final thrust deep inside, gripping my hips as he plunges and simultaneously tramping his thumb on my clit.

I come so hard I feel like I'm losing consciousness.

Deep warmth spreads inside me as his release bathes my womb with his seed and we pulse together.

We stay locked like that, and Wrings spreads his body over mine like a flesh-wrapped steel cocoon of heat and protection.

His eyes never leave my face. He whispers one word, and my nod is shy.

Mine.

☠

I wrap my arms around Shannon's fragile body and briefly wonder why she's so thin.

Gonna fatten her up first thing.

"Got your cast drenched," I mention, stroking her long silky hair out of her face.

"I don't care," Shannon says in a languid voice.

"Good damn thing." I kiss her temple then frown. "Hey, I'm sorry."

She turns in my arms, and her right breast sort of falls into my hand. I mound the soft flesh with my fingers and kiss the tip of her light-pink nipple. It hardens against my lips.

"Why are you sorry?" Shannon asks in a breathy voice, arching into my caress.

My exhale is soft. "Not good with words. Just sort of stole you away from your life and forced you—"

Shannon puts her fingers on my mouth. "No," she begins in a low voice, "I'm the one who's sorry. I mean…" Her eyes drift from mine, and only an ancient nightlight plugged into the wall behind us shows me any part of her expression. Regret is etched on her features. "My mom kept telling me to improve our lives by getting rid of the house and getting more hours, pursuing a career."

I put a finger on her chin and turn her to face me again, wrapping part of the sheet around her body.

"Mom knows she's dying. And she's been encouraging me to live. I just haven't found a good enough reason to."

"Vincent's dead," I remind her.

One Blood tormenter down. The entire gang to go. *Fuck.*

She slowly nods. "He's gone."

Shannon trembles in my arms, and I tighten my hold. "But now there's Lopez—and I had this Realtor come by the house, and he's working for them. If I sell the house now, the only people who'll buy it is one of those gang losers."

My feelings swell as I listen to her problems. They're mine, too, now. I admit quietly, "I don't have much to offer."

She touches me, and I go hard.

"You have something to offer, Wring." Her smile is sly.

I cock my head. "Not very virginal, Shannon," I tease. It's worth it to make out her blush in the gloom of the bedroom.

"True, but I'm not one anymore." She smiles. "But when it comes to us—and whatever we have here—I don't care."

Shannon sits up suddenly. "My mom." Her eyes fill with anxiety.

"Storm's there."

Her pale-blond eyebrow rises, silvered in the oblique moonlight cast through the old window. "How do you know?"

"Checked my cell as I got off my ride. Hell—we were too busy to check before then." I give a lopsided smile and the low light from the nightlight showcases the deepening red on her cheeks.

"She okay?" She bites her bottom lip between her teeth.

I nod. "Storm's dumber than a box of rocks, but he's a solid guy. Gonna be a brother soon." *Helluva lot sooner than Trainer,* I think with a smirk.

Shannon falls back against the pillows, and I prop up on an elbow, crossing my ankles. Could use a smoke about now.

"Come on." I hold out my hand.

Shannon takes it, and I tow her behind me to the bathroom. I put a washcloth under warm running water then wring out the excess water, placing it on the rim of the sink. Turning, I put my hands at her waist and boost her on top of the vanity.

"Wring!" she squeals, giggling.

Love the way her face looks right then. Happy. "Hang on, gonna clean you."

The corners of her mouth lift. "I think you've done a fine job of it."

I roll my eyes to look at her, already between those fine thighs. "A man doesn't take a girl's virginity then do nothing to take care of her later."

"Oh," she says, her voice small.

I stop, washcloth in hand, and stare at her. "Hey, I mean it. Let me take care of you, Shannon."

She puts her hand on mine and squeezes. "You already have. Crude and brash, tender and hard, you take care of every part of me, Wring."

I nod. She's got it.

I get to work, cleaning her gorgeous slit of my cum and her blood. Hymen or not, I'm washing the proof of her innocence away forever.

It wasn't stolen by the fucking gangbangers, but taken by a guy that's falling for her like a ton of bricks.

"What is this place?" I ask Wring, looking out over the jagged landscape. Rolling hills with spears of dark trees surround the driveway. The road beyond is a ribbon of shadow.

He sits in his tight boxer briefs, smoking a cigarette while I admire his stomach muscles bunching with his small movements. The tip of the cigarette glows like a small torch as he takes a drag.

His feet land on the wood porch as he puts the cigarette out. "Road Kill MC prez's place. He's letting me use it while my house is being built."

I feel my eyebrows rise. "You're getting a house built?"

He nods, folding his hands behind his head. "Yeah, out by my brother, Snare. Orting." He grunts when he sees my face. "Don't looks so surprised."

I laugh, thinking I'd definitely been a little judgey.

Wring's eyes cruise my expression. "Come 'ere."

I stand and shuffle away from the rocking chair where I'd been sitting, holding a fluffy blanket covering my nudity.

"What put that look on your face. Because"—he looks up at me then pulls me down on his lap as his face goes low—"I love the look I put on your face when I make you come."

Heat rises to my cheeks, and I fight not to touch them. "But I like this look, too." He runs a finger down my hot skin, and I lean into the caress.

"I like the country," I say simply, remembering my parent's conversations of a once-rural Kent. Riding horses. Watching shapes in clouds under the protection of towering trees. The smell of clover in the summer. The sound of crickets as autumn approaches. Or the wind through the trees. A wistful sigh parts my lips.

"Me, too," he confesses.

We sit for a time, me safe in Wring's arms.

"What was that thing you did to Lopez?" I finally ask softly.

He chuckles in the darkness that shrouds the place so heavily. "Which part?"

"The rope stuff. You and Noose—and—Lariat?" I ask, not sure if I got the guy's name right.

"That's right."

"You guys have funny names."

"The name my parents gave me is Sam Walker."

"Sam," I muse then shake my head. "Can't see you that way now."

"Wring's my road name. Name we go by in the club."

In my head, I tick off the names I've heard him mention. Noose, Snare, Lariat, and Wring. There's something about them all…I'm missing the connection. "What do they mean?"

He gives me a sidelong look. "Not into question and answer, Shannon."

I stiffen a little. *Well, excuse me.* I cross my arms, wrapping myself tighter within the blanket. "I just gave you my virginity inside of knowing you about a week. You know *everything* about me. I'm entitled to answers, Wring."

He frowns, his features intense. "That's where you're wrong, sweetheart. You're not entitled to dick. Anything I give you, I give you because I want you to have it. Not because you demand shit."

I feel like crying. Wring had been so tender with me. So vital. So protective. But I ask a few questions, and he's running from the answers.

Like he has something to hide.

Suddenly, I don't feel so safe in his arms. I feel spent. Tired. Uncertain.

I move to stand, and his hold tightens.

"I don't talk. It's not who I am, Shannon."

I know my expression is fierce as I look at him. "Well, I'm taking a huge risk here, Wring."

"And I'm not? I stuck my nose in where it didn't belong. I protected a girl marked by the Bloods. Road Kill has been carefully negotiating territory and all kinds of other bullshit. Now I've blown it all to hell—for you. Forgive me if I don't just puke out my life's story."

I lift my chin. "Why then? You said I wasn't special."

"Ya are. I just couldn't admit it."

Okay.

"Noose, Lariat, and me were in Afghanistan together, SEAL teammates. Patched in to the club after. None of us could be citizens again after fighting for our country. Had to do our own thing, on our own terms."

"The names...they're all—"

"We're knotters. Expert knotters."

I pull away, looking at his face. It's void of expression. In the darkness of the porch and surrounding woods, I can see nothing of what he feels.

I know a little bit about Navy SEALs. "You mean assassins?" I ask in a voice that's icy calm.

His eyes are serious, not budging an inch. "What me and the guys did while serving. That's not something we're ever gonna talk about. Ever."

My heart sinks. *I can't be with a man who's a killer.* What does it matter that he did it for America? I saw what he did to those gangbangers back there. What he could do with a length of rope.

I let Wring's protection cloud my judgement. My lust for him led me into a bigger mess than what I have with the gang.

How could I be so dumb?

"Okay," I say, my voice is hollow.

"Let's get to bed. Gonna be a long damn day tomorrow."

He stands, easily lifting me in his arms.

Carrying me into the bed, he unwraps me like a gift and climbs in next to me.

Wring holds me in his arms and falls asleep almost instantly.

I don't sleep for a long time.

15

I wake up with a start, feeling my chest, thighs, and head. *What the fuck?*

I look around and squint at the vaguely illuminated hands of the clock.

One o'clock.

Holy *shit*. That means I slept for ten hours straight.

I look beside me. Shannon's gone, but the side of the bed where she slept is still warm.

Where is she?

And a better question: how did her being beside me help me rest? And not kind of rest. I slept like the dead. Feel fucking swell.

Swinging my legs out of bed, I stand then walk to the bathroom and take a leak. I saunter out to the kitchen and fill a glass of water from the spring-fed aqua system Vipe's got out here, my eyes scanning the cabin's interior.

No sign of Shannon.

Hmmm. I stride to the bed and wrench my jeans on. I grab the rope that I always have on my nightstand and stuff it, knot first, in my left-hand front pocket.

Tearing open the front door, I survey the landscape with a narrow gaze. "Shannon!" I bellow.

Nothing but birds, bees, and breeze.

Fuck.

I think back on our little chat from the night before. She didn't seem to warm up on my lack of chatty. Never tried for anything past a quick lay with most chicks. New to this relationship garbage.

And I've never dealt with the virginity thing. Never had to. Sweet butts sure aren't fucking virgins by the time they're servicing the club. Everybody's been in those cracks.

Maybe I should have shared more with Shannon. Hate fucking sharing. Chatting it up is for guys who want to grow their own uteruses.

Not feeling *that*. I snort, slamming the door, and charge headlong for my cell.

Jamming out a text to Noose, I realize I didn't see a cell anywhere near Shannon, and I pause mid-tap.

She must have one, right? Most girls have a text in their hand likes it's part of them.

I've never seen her with one.

I hit Send.

Noose pings me right back: *Hey man, I apologize. I had nothing to do with it.*

I sit up straighter, hit the little symbol for mic, and talk into my phone. I'm a fucking fanny fat finger when it comes to texting.

Me: What do ya mean?

Noose: Fuck man, Rose got a call from your girl, Shannon—to come pick her up from Viper's place. I wasn't here, she sort of stealthed the whole deal.

Raw heat kicks on from deep inside me, a sucker-punch of licking flames.

Me: She's in a fuckton of danger. What with Lopez around the damn corner and only Storm to watch her.

Noose: Storm's not on detail. Viper's got him doing other stuff. You had her so he took off after she got back to take care of her mom.

Me: Get over there, Noose, I'll be right there.

Noose: Man—hate to be the bearer of the shit news but your girl's not interested. Told Rose she doesn't want to be with a murderer.

My head tips back, and I chew off a holler that rattles the glass.

How could Shannon misunderstand me that much? I'm not a danger to her—I'm a danger to others who would hurt her. *Fuck.*

I jump up, rip my shirt on inside out, and grab my cell one-handed as I toss my boots on without zipping them. I stomp to my ride.

My cell buzzes, and I see it's Noose calling.

"Yeah?" I bark into the phone as I sit on my ride and start it up. Jamming a smoke in my mouth for good measure, I balance the phone between my shoulder and ear.

"Hate fucking texting. Auto correct slays the words, man."

I roll my eyes, taking a deep drag. "Shannon's making me a fucking insane-asylum candidate."

Noose chuckles.

"Fuck you," I say.

"Uh-huh. I said a lot of that last year."

"I'm going. I don't need your bullshit. Gotta get to her, straighten shit out."

"Yeah." There's a pause in the conversation, eaten by the noise of my bike as I cruise down the dirt road. "Sorry Rose got involved. And Wring?"

"Yeah," I bite, looking both left and right before I head west toward Shannon's.

"I looked into her more. Shannon and her mom are two, almost three, years behind in their property taxes. They've got a land line but no cell phone."

Knew it.

"What are you saying? 'Cause I can't talk." The bike's drowning Noose's words even though he's shouting.

"She's poor as fuck," he yells.

"That's why she's so skinny," I say mainly to myself.

"What?" Noose bellows into the cell and I wince. "Never mind. See ya soon. Get your ass over there."

I can almost hear the sigh.

"Affirmative, fucker."

Grinning, I slide my phone between the handlebars, relaxing as I put on the speed, hurtling toward Shannon.

For the first time in forever, a sense of impending loss looms.

I find I've got something to lose.

Rose covers my hand as a cooing baby serenades us.

"I feel like such a weasel," she says, squeezing my hand.

Me, too. But it's the only way. A clean break. Wring shouldn't shoulder the burden of my life. He got me out of that mess—two messes—but I don't want to put him in the position to have to kill people. And I have a feeling he will.

"This is super fucking sneaky," Rose says.

I take in my surroundings. The driveway to the cabin is probably a half mile, which I walked. My jeans were salvageable, as was my bra—but the gore-encrusted shirt was toast.

I left it in the trash and grabbed a shirt—probably Wring's, since it fit me like a dress—and wore that. I walked half the length of the driveway then jogged the rest.

The entire time, I had a feeling that Wring would wake up and come after me.

He didn't. Never seen anyone sleep so soundly. Almost like he didn't have a care in the world—or hadn't slept in such a long time that he was desperate for sleep.

"I know it's kind of crappy of me." I look at the hand Rose was just holding as she pulls onto the highway leading home.

"Well…"

"I just—he doesn't want to talk, and you should have seen him and Noose—"

"I have," Rose says quietly, gripping the wheel so hard her knuckles whiten. "There's nothing scarier than Noose using knots."

173

I swallow. *Except Wring using them.*

"The skills he learned in the military are the only things that kept him alive," Rose's large brown eyes look at me, and she finishes in a low voice, "and me."

I shrug. "I don't need that level of violence in my life. I have enough to figure out with my home situation, I can't...address that too."

"For what it's worth, I don't think Wring would ever be violent with women."

I glance at her while she's driving. "That's not it. I have my mom, and I have to protect her, too. I can't have Wring making things worse with the gangbangers."

"Seems to me it'd be worse if he and Noose hadn't figured it out."

I sigh. "Yeah, I do make some stupid decisions, but at this point, I think he's more of a catalyst for antagonizing them."

"I wouldn't live one minute without Noose's protection. He absolutely keeps us safe." She sounds so convicted, and that's great for her. She's married, with a baby. Different situation.

Her smile is a twisted lip lift of irony. "I know what you're thinking, Shannon."

Tight breath releases in a tired sigh. "I'm thinking that my mom needs food and her meds."

"No—stop thinking about your mom. You've already told me that she can got to the bathroom and get basic things. You don't need to be there every second, Shannon."

Rose's right. But if she *is* right, why does being away from the constancy of Mom's care feel so wrong?

"Wring is smoother than Noose."

I swing my head to her, and she glances my way, barking out a laugh when she catches sight of my expression of clear surprise. "Really?"

"I can't believe it. I mean, if there was a nickel for every F-bomb uttered—"

"Every reference to the golden hoo-hah."

I laugh, nodding. "Yeah, the guys seem pretty obsessive." I blush, thinking about what Wring did to my body just hours ago.

"Whoa, look at that face."

"Num-num!" Baby Aria shouts from the back seat, and I jump a foot.

Rose cringes. "Sorry about that. She's got a real appetite, and she's not afraid to let us know."

At her words, my stomach growls. I do mental inventory of groceries in the house and come up empty. Gnawing continues in my belly. But I know from experience that the hunger will quiet if I just ignore it. For a couple of hours.

"Hungry?" Rose's eyebrow quirks.

I lift a shoulder. "Not so much."

"You're bone thin, Shannon."

I ignore her, looking out the window.

"We can get burgers. I know this great place that makes banana-peanut-butter-chocolate milkshakes."

My stomach lets out a walloping howl.

Rose laughs. "Huh. Let's go there."

"I don't need charity."

Rose hits me in the arm, and I flinch, turning to her in anger.

But my anger fades as she smiles. "Aria's hungry. You wouldn't say no to a hungry baby, would you?"

I shake my head. "You're sort of violent, too," I grump, rubbing my arm.

"When the need calls for it," she replies cryptically and turns in to a dive of a burger place.

I try not to wolf down my food, especially when Rose ignored my attempt to order a kid's meal.

"Are you a kid? No. A grown woman needs more than three hundred and fifty calories a day."

Relenting, I take another slurp of my delicious shake and shift on the rickety picnic bench. It groans under my weight, lurching under my butt. I clutch the sides of my frozen cup.

"This place has been here since my folks were kids," Rose says, looking around at the steep parking lot that flows into the tiny, flat-roofed building, then pops a fry into Aria's mouth.

She thoughtfully takes it out, mashes it between her fingers and smears it between her lips.

Adorable.

My fries are long gone, and only two bites of my burger remain. A pang of guilt slices through me, thinking about my mom alone with only yogurt and bread for toast in our fridge.

I push the burger basket away.

Hot tears run down my face as I choke down the rest of my shake.

"God, Shannon, what is it? Please…" She reaches for my hand across the rough wood table.

Aria whimpers in apparent sympathy then screams, "Num-num!"

I smile through my tears.

Rose absently offers her another fry, and I give her my best, albeit shaky, answer while squeezing her hand back. "I can't…I don't have any money." I let go of her hand and sink my face into my palms, hiding my face.

Rose makes sure Aria is busy and latched in the high chair before she rushes around to my side of the table. "I know, Shannon. It's okay."

"It isn't, Rose. I can't pay our taxes and buy enough food, and I can't work more hours because Mom needs care."

Rose strokes my back. "Let Wring take care of you, Shannon."

I lift my tear-stained face to hers. "For how long, Rose? Until the next girl comes along?"

Rose's smile is a little sad at the edges. "Those MC guys can have any woman they want, any time. They don't need girls like us." She jabs her thumb into her chest.

The baby screams again, just to hear her own voice. Our faces whip in her direction, and Aria gives us a devastating smile, a single dimple flashing in her pudgy cheek.

I turn back to Shannon, eyebrows knitting. "Like what?"

Rose grins, tapping my nose. "Complicated." She sighs. "If Wring wants a slut-ho to stick his wick in, they're a dime a dozen."

I blink at her description, food churning in my stomach at her words.

Rose guffaws.

Aria screams, "Num-num!" swinging a defiant arm at the sky. Rose gives her another fry. "Pig," she says then adds, "oink-oink." Aria wrinkles her nose and tries to make the pig noise.

"That's not going to be attractive when she's older, you know," I say, but I'm smiling.

"That's okay. Less guys for Noose to beat the shit out of for looking at his baby girl."

The moment swells, me thinking about rough men and the women who love them.

"Thank you for lunch," I say quietly.

Rose takes my hand again, and Aria pitches a mangled fry on the pavement.

"Thanks for being there for Wring."

I frown. I'm not *there*.

Rose nods. "He's been different in the week he's known you."

I raise an eyebrow, not understanding. "How so?"

She pats my hand, unhooks Aria from the confines of the high chair, and hikes her on a hip. "Not sure. Whole, maybe?"

"Whole?" I give a small laugh, standing and stretching. Wring's huge T-shirt comes to mid-thigh, and a pleasant throb between my thighs reminds me of what I've done.

Loved.

"Yeah," she says, a wistful catch in her voice, "those guys come back from war, and they're not them anymore." She looks at me. "Sometimes it takes just the right woman to heal all their hurts."

Maybe for both of us.

16

I roll up to Shannon's driveway and immediately see the door is ajar.

Splintered at the jamb.

Cold dread spreads from the center of me out to my extremities.

The numb slips away. I feel everything then. Things I don't want to.

Some things, I do.

The bulge of my Colt .45 at my ankle. The sweet tightness of my knotted end of rope at my hip. The succulent sting of adrenaline piercing me like a lit up Christmas tree of Swiss cheese.

Everything is where it needs to be as I dismount in a hopping slide over the top of my seat.

I leave the hog running.

Sliding along the siding, I hear someone tossing the house.

One of my eyeballs cruises around the edge of the torn doorjamb. Gangbangers crawl over the interior of Shannon's modest house like ants.

I move fully into the threshold, ripping the gun from my holster in a whispering tear of fabric. "Hey, fucknuts," I greet in a cheerful tone.

They turn, hands full of jewelry and things that glint in the afternoon light piercing the window pane.

I snag a pillow from a nearby recliner and put it in front of the muzzle of my piece.

"Fuck!" one of them shouts.

They drop what they're holding, raising their own weapons.

The gun has a slight kick as I fire, and a red bloom opens in the center of the first gangbanger's surprised face.

I pivot my gun slightly to the right and pull the trigger again.

A flower of blood opens in the cheekbone of the second man. Skull fragments and pillow guts fly like scattered clouds of torn gauze. The details of their death appear as a vapor of smoke moving between us.

I chuck the pillow and walk over to the bodies.

A thin silver-toned necklace is still wrapped around the finger of one of them. The digit twitches.

Bending over, I unwind it from his lifeless finger and pocket it. I pluck my cell from the pocket of my cut and sweep a thumb over the encryption.

My page surfaces inside the glass rectangle, my heated gun still in my left hand, and I hit the speech-to-text icon and speak. "Clean up, Aisle Thirteen."

Noose's answering ping is instant: *Affirmative. ETA five minutes.*

I wait as my gun cools, then walk over to the ruined door. I work on trying to close it for a few minutes, hiking it up and sort of hitching it into place. *Fuck it.* I give up. The panel hangs off hinges like a shattered wooden tooth.

Noose's bike and two others come to park beside mine.

He saunters to the door, meeting my eyes through the space of the obliterated door and jamb. He nods in wordless greeting, and I sweep a palm toward the interior.

Noose's eyes land on the two gangbangers with a dispassionate glance. "Where's the mother?" There are a million other questions to ask.

He forms the only one that truly matters.

"Don't know," I admit.

The two prospects go over to the bodies, lift them up by the pits, and start dragging them to the adjacent garage.

Noose and I survey the squiggly blood trails left behind by their heels.

Noose folds his arms, shooting his chin up. "Park those fucks in the garage. We'll do hearse detail at night." His fingers ghost over his pocket for cigarettes. "Fuck—need a smoke."

Storm grunts, hauling the first body through the door threshold and slumping it against the wall.

Noose chuckles. "No, Storm—ya dumb fuck. R.I.G.O.R. That'll set in, and he'll be an *L* we can't get into another letter. You feel me?" Noose puts a hand to his chest and goes on, "Flat on his back. We'll plank his ass into the truck with a tarp and make them both go away. Stack 'em like sardines if we have to." He chuckles.

The corners of my lips tweak. Noose has always been the most pragmatic of us SEALs.

Storm nods, heaving the dead dude onto the middle of a carless garage floor. What's left of his head makes a dull thunk as it claps hard against the concrete.

The other prospect—don't know his name yet—lurches his corpse beside the other one.

"Cover 'em," Noose says, swirling his hand in a circle like that should have been obvious to them.

Storm shakes out a blue tarp neatly folded in a corner, and it floats down like an electric-blue shroud, covering the bodies.

Noose turns to me. "Report."

I tell him.

"Heard from Rose. She's got your girl."

My shoulders ease in relief. I don't deny she's not mine anymore. Shannon couldn't be any less mine if I tried to disconnect.

I'm so connected.

"Snare's gonna be steaming pissed," Noose says with a rough exhale. He swipes his hand over the crown of his head, using a hairband to tie his longish hair back.

"Yeah," I say, "couldn't be helped. Had to cancel those fuckers."

He sweeps a palm wide. "They're gonna be missed, Wring. Ya know it, man."

I shrug. "Either way, Shannon's mom isn't here, and she's unwell."

"She's probably dead."

I let my anguish—Shannon's borrowed anguish—out through my nose, suck in another breath, hold it in my lungs, and release. "Yup."

"You thinking she's your property now?" Noose is too decent to let the *I told you so* inside his tone of voice.

"Yeah," I admit quietly.

"Don't think she knows that yet," Noose cackles then snorts, "Not like that mattered with Rose. Knew she was mine, took her, knocked her up—put the rock on her finger." He lifts a shoulder as punctuation then digs around in the front pocket of his cut for a smoke, and scowls when he comes up empty.

A hard laugh shoots out of me, and I murmur sarcastically, "Don't think that'll work with Shannon."

"Try it," Noose says, digging around in another pocket and finding a smoke. He lights up, shooting a ring in the middle of Shannon's trashed living room. His flinty eyes slide to mine, narrow and hard. "You might like it."

He winks, and we walk out the front door.

The prospects will erase our presence. We've trained them how. We left a DNA trail that couldn't be missed; it's a mile wide.

Fire cleanses everything.

I'm already apologizing to Shannon. But some things can't be helped.

Like the Bloods and their interest in my property. And what my property loves.

They'll fucking pay.

Come to think of it, they already have. I'm just calling their debt due.

"They'll expect retaliation." Viper's voice is a dull flat sound like words dropping in a hollow bucket.

"We don't want war, Viper," Noose says, "but they drew first blood."

"Like Rambo," Trainer says, eyebrows popping high.

We both look at him across the table of emergency church. "Just saying."

"Don't," I seethe.

"Your girl is safe at Noose's, true?"

We nod.

"You just got a text from Rose?" Viper says, part in question. "Shannon might have decided she wasn't wanting to be your girl, but your girl's safe. Got to prioritize. Her safe is better than anything I can think of." His near-translucent gaze turns to me, "But her mom isn't a club priority."

"I've thrown down for her," I comment, rock solid.

Viper nods. "Miracles never cease. But you need to see it from my perspective. Gotta ton of reluctant fucking property lately. Got Noose's girl—Rose—did everything but hang a sign around her neck that said *fuck off*." A bark of laughter breaks loose. "Clearly, Noose didn't." His clear pool water gaze pegs Noose, and he ducks his head. "Then we have my sergeant-at-arms chasing sissy around—"

Snare stands, and Viper puts up a palm, snickering. "Sorry, Snare. Sometimes you grab humor where it presents itself. I know you guys aren't actually related anymore."

"Because mother fucking Riker is dead," Snare says slowly at our Road Kill Prez, like his cheese just slid off his cracker. Then Snare adds, "Thank fuck."

Viper leans back. "Now we've got yet another potential old lady that somehow"—his astute gaze crawls over my face—"manages to live in the middle of gangland."

He throws his hands up and slams his palms flat on the table.

None of us jump.

He glares at Noose and me. "And you had the two prospects torch a house after you cleaned a couple of Bloods—who *will* be missed at some point. And believe me, Lopez will not buy into it being an accidental blaze. Not that I mind two less Bloods. It's timing, gentlemen."

"Fire seemed simpler in the end," Noose explains in a vacant voice.

Viper glowers at the fifteen faces around the long rectangular slab of wood that serves as our meeting place. His steely gaze never leaves me. "Fuck it. Find out if Shannon will be your property. I can't give club support behind an unwilling female. I just can't. If the Bloods had Shannon"—Viper spreads his hands—"I'd take the risk for potential property of a brother. But for the almost-dead, arthritic mom?" He exhales roughly. "It's cowardly as fuck those Bloods would take a sick old lady as bait and hostage fodder, but that's what separates us from them. We're unwilling to exploit those who are defenseless—and they are. We can't save every hard-luck case. Even if she deserves to be saved."

All eyes go to Noose as he leans forward suddenly, a lit cell in his hand.

"What?" I ask, knowing it's bad from the absolutely blank expression on his face.

"Rose isn't answering my text."

"Maybe Aria's going down for a nap?" I hate the hope in my tone.

"Nah," Trainer says, leaning back in his chair, "probably took one of those blast-it-out-the-back-of-the-diaper shits. Rose is busy on clean-up duty, I bet." He smirks.

Noose gives him a murderous look, and his face falls.

"Fuck, just a joke, man," Trainer mutters, throwing his palms up.

Noose flips him off then says to the room of brothers, "Don't like it."

Snare's eyebrow hikes. "She good about getting back?"

Noose's nod is thoughtful. He looks at the prospect pair who remain. Storm and the other nameless guy are busy setting Shannon's house on fire. *She's going to hate me.*

I turn to Noose. "You got security up the keister at your place."

Noose nods. "It's only as good as the door. If anyone—" Noose tears the tie out of his hair and snaps the elastic ring between his fingers like a rubber band.

An uneasy, bloated silence fills the space where we breathe. I'm suddenly fighting for oxygen as different scenarios fill my already-crowded head.

"Meeting adjourned." Viper hits the gavel to the circular wood placard. The look he gives me is iron compassion. "Find out." He points at me then swings his finger at Noose. "Go figure out why your old lady isn't getting back with you."

"It's probably nothing." Noose shrugs, every bit of him on edge.

Lariat, the quietest of us all, pipes up for the first time. "She was at the condo, right? When she texted they got home."

Noose nods.

Lariat keeps his dark eyes on Noose. "You got a feeling?"

Noose nods again, hands clenching into fists. "Yup."

Lariat shrugs. "Good enough for me."

My heartbeats tick faster. *Shannon's with Rose and Aria.* I've got to believe Noose is being overprotective and freaking out about nothing.

But our experience wasn't like that in the sandbox. His Spidey sense was damn unnerving. The skill saved our fucking asses.

Viper comes up to me and Noose and grabs us around the necks, though we kind of dwarf him. "Listen, you Nancys, go check on the women. Get shit figured out. Then call me. No texting bullshit—can't figure that tech out. We'll go from there. We finally got shit settled with Chaos. An uneasy truce is better than no truce."

Snare adds, "And the cop is on the inside with Chaos Riders."

"Puck?" I clarify.

Noose is already heading for the door, with me on his heels.

"Yeah," Snare says.

"Fucked-up road name. He couldn't pick any better than that?" Viper says randomly.

Snare shrugs. "Canadian. And whatever—that's the guy's real name—nickname."

"You guys go." Viper tilts his head with a flick toward Snare and Lariat. "Just in case Noose's gut is real instead of nerves."

Noose grabs the door before it can swing shut and shoots a look at Prez. "I don't get nerves."

That's more true than anything I've heard in a week.

17

"You really think I should disregard this violent streak that Wring has?" I ask Rose as we ascend in the elevator on the way to her condo.

She shakes her head, and I'm momentarily surprised. "No—I, don't disregard what he is. Just…accept him."

Aria lays her head on Rose's shoulder, giving me a glassy, thousand-mile stare.

I smile and flutter my fingers.

She gives me a sleepy wave back.

Cutie.

"It's super-close to naptime," Rose says apologetically.

My eyes rise from the nearly sleeping baby. "That's no problem. I love kids." Mist covers my eyes, and I close them, ruthlessly keeping my sadness at bay.

"What, Shannon?"

The elevator rocks as it comes to a stop. The doors whisper open, and I step out. Rose follows.

"I—it sounds so selfish, but if my mom wasn't so compromised physically, I would have gone to school, become an elementary teacher. I've always loved kids."

"Charlie loves you at story time."

I'm sure my smile is wistful. "Yeah," I say softly. "They're sort of like my own kids." I think of Sally, and that causes me a pang of anxiety.

"Maybe once you hook up with Wring, you'll have more options."

I turn to her, and we're standing right outside her door. "I don't want to 'hook up' with Wring. I mean—" I feel my blush from my toes to my scalp. "We have hooked up. I want to end it, or I want more. A ton more."

Rose nods. "I understand. But Wring has problems since he's been back from the war," she confides, "ya know—emotionally. He doesn't sleep well."

I can't help it. I cover the giggle with a hand.

Her eyebrows arch, and she shifts Aria to the other shoulder. The baby's eyes are drooping so hard, they're tiny slivers of chocolate in her face.

"He sleeps just fine," I say.

"Really?"

I nod. "Like the dead."

Rose grins. "So either you wore him out"—she pauses significantly, her lips quirking at the corners—"or you make him feel better. Safe."

I feel my face tighten in disbelief. "I can't make an aggressive killer feel safe. He's the one that makes *me* feel safe," I say with quiet emphasis.

"That's it, though, Shannon. Don't you see it? You make each other feel safe."

I lift a shoulder. Maybe she's on to something.

Rose touches my arm. "Please tell me you won't shut Wring out without giving him a chance."

Her big brown eyes look into mine.

I nod. "Okay."

Rose turns, and I hear her word before her hand goes to the doorknob. "Good."

Then Rose is screaming as she's wrenched inside her condo.

Aria's startled cry greets my ears, and I don't run.

I can't abandon them.

Even though Lopez's eyes drill into me through the open doorway.

His intent is like an advertisement.

"Come here, virgin bitch."

My stomach does a slick, slow roll. The delicious shake threatens to dive back up my throat.

I'm no virgin.

Another gangbanger has Rose, his arms wrapped around her.

I gulp back my fear. There's more than me in this scenario.

"Don't hurt my baby, please," Rose says, tears streaming down her face.

Another gangbanger holds a wailing Aria by the waist, legs and arms dangling.

My gaze swings to Lopez. *Oh God, oh God, oh God.*

"Well, that depends," Lopez says, his eyes shifting to mine. "If your friend cooperates, then we leave you two bitches here." His eyes sweep over the baby, and icy dread slithers down my spine. "The little bitch and the big bitch." He laughs, reaching out. He grabs Rose's large breast and mounds it, tweaking the nipple.

She mewls, turning her head away. "Noose will kill you if you hurt us," she says through her fear.

He twists her nipple, and she screams. The baby hollers louder, sympathetic terror causing her eyes to leap from one gangbanger to the other.

The gangbanger shakes her.

"I'll do it!" I scream above their cries.

"What will you do, Shannon?" Lopez says with soft menace.

"Anything," I answer instantly. "Just leave Rose and the baby alone."

Lopez smiles. "Dump the kid in a crib somewhere and tie up the cunt."

The gangbanger stalks into all the rooms, and Rose clutches the arms that hold her, every bit of her body straining toward her crying child.

He comes out empty-handed. "Got the little bitch where she belongs. Kiddie prison." As he smirks, the teardrop tattoos on his cheek rise with the insincere lift of lips.

"Now you're coming with us. We got a surprise for you, too."

I don't like how he says "surprise," and my heart begins to thump.

"Shannon," Rose calls out, and the gangbanger backhands her.

"Don't," Lopez says. "If we don't do anything to his woman, we can still be in the clear."

The guy hauls Rose to her feet. He scrapes a kitchen chair away from the same table I ate pancakes at and sets it behind her. A heavy hand on her shoulder thumps her in place.

He extracts zip ties from his pocket and locks her ankles and hands into place with a ripping sound of plastic.

Lopez approaches, and Rose cowers. "You tell your man to stay out of it. Or I let my boys that don't have any conscious come over and work you over." His eyes move to the other end of the house, where Aria screams from her crib, and he adds, "And the kid."

Rose blanches then nods robotically, while fresh tears drip off her chin and onto her hands.

"You'll wish you were dead by the time we're done with you." His hungry gaze moves to her breasts, and Rose bravely stares him down.

"I'd have fun fucking you, Road Kill property." He licks his lips and folds his arms, looking down at her. "Be smart, protect your daughter."

"What about Shannon?" Rose asks with soft insistence.

I shut my eyes. *God.*

"Forget her. Shannon's a ghost. You know, something you say you saw, and no one believes."

He wraps his hand around my bicep. His thumb touches his forefinger. "Come on," he hisses in my ear and takes me out of Rose's.

Leading me down the hall, he comes to the fire exit door and a snarling mess of wires, obviously the result of disabling the alarm, hang from an electrical panel.

The gangbangers follow us.

As do the cries of a little girl and her mama.

Noose races up the escape ladder to the condo.

Elevator's out of commission.

His long strides eat the treads like candy, and Lariat, Snare, and I follow.

He grips the metal rails on either side and blasts in the emergency exit door with a well-placed shitkicker.

Female cries reach my ears, and Noose sprints through the open door without checking his points.

I guess if my wife and child were in peril, I would charge in, too.

Whipping around through the open door, I catch sight of Rose. She's gagged with a Blood bandana, and tears have soaked it.

Noose is not with her, and I go to her, taking my folding blade from my front pocket, and cut the ties at the hands.

Her eyes move behind me.

I duck. The whistle of my utility blade is the only sound as I whirl in a three-sixty, burying the blade into the gut of a gangbanger.

His eyes round in surprise.

If they'd done their homework, they would understand how dumb their methods are.

If I weren't in my head, I would have looked at my weak spots before entering.

Neither of us did. Shows how gone we are on the girls. How careless we are.

I thrust the blade up, and though small, weapons are liquid in my hands, following the extension of my will like a part of my body.

His guts, a steamy mess of glistening pearly worms, tumble to the floor.

Rose starts puking.

I turn.

His hand grabs my ankle as his other tries to hold his guts inside his body.

"Persistent fucker," I say from the casual place I go when I kill.

I sweep the sharp blade down, sawing through his seeking fingers without much trouble.

The digits fall like decapitated flesh trees on the floor.

Rose tries to get away, and the chair tips.

I catch it with my gory hand and right it.

Squatting beside her feet, I begin to cut off the zip ties there. She screams in a blast of raw terror that takes me back to the Middle East.

I've heard that sound. It's like a bellowing alarm of impending death.

Wild-eyed, Noose charges into the room, carrying little Aria, who's hiccupping back sobs.

"What the righteous fuck?" he yells, checking out the carnage.

"Cutting the wife loose," I reply evenly, though my fingers tremble just the slightest bit from the noise that Rose made.

What do they call my reaction? Oh yeah, post-traumatic stress or some clinical shit like that.

"Hey, baby—it's going to be okay," Noose says in a soothing voice, taking a step toward her.

Then he steps on a finger. He looks down, raises an eyebrow at me, and kicks it aside.

Noose glowers.

"Hey, man, didn't check your corners, just came charging in. I had some clean up here."

We exchange a glance.

"'Kay." Noose looks at Rose.

She's staring off into space.

"God, baby—I'm so sorry."

Aria begins to cry then wraps her arms around her dad's neck.

Rose breaks, great hitching sobs cutting the space like knives. She stands, but her knees buckle, and Noose catches her, whispering words I can't hear.

Rose shakes her head, tears flying from her cheeks.

"Ya gotta, baby." Noose cradles her face, and Lariat comes in, holding out his arms.

"Let me take the munchkin." Noose hands her off, and I walk to Rose.

"Rose."

She turns in my direction, new tears flowing over the tracks of the last. "I can't, Wring."

She turns to Noose. "He said he'd come back here and…" Rose's hands clench. "Hurt Aria."

Noose sucks in a breath. "Nobody's hurting my family, Rose."

She leans back, her head tipping back. "Noose, they got inside somehow."

His hand slaps the table so hard, the wood cracks. "The fucking emergency escape was wired. They had someone undo it—the only weakness."

"If they can get in once, they can get in again. Gotta booby trap this place to death," Snare says.

"Yeah. Duh," Noose says, incinerating him with a glance.

"Where is Shannon?" I ask.

All eyes turn to me.

Noose looks back at Rose, hauling her against him. "They didn't hurt Aria. I'm pissed as fuck they broke in here, but they didn't really do anything but scare you."

"I'm terrified, Noose." Rose wipes away her tears. "Does this mean you won't kill them, Noose—that we can just ignore them?"

I grin.

Noose gives an almost imperceptible shake of his head. "No, baby. They're all gonna die. They threatened my family." The pitch of his voice lowers to a growl. "They touched our daughter. We're lucky Charlie was with your parents." He lifts her chin with a finger. "And as sure as I'm standing here, I bet that Lopez couldn't keep his hands off my property."

His eyes search her face.

"Yes," she admits in the barest thread of a whisper.

"See?" he lifts his shoulders, releasing her chin.

Rose grips the collar of his cut, crunching the leather. "Don't, Noose. Shannon went with them so we wouldn't be hurt."

"And what kind of man would I be if I didn't go and get her back—Wring?"

She looks at me. "I'm so sorry."

I shake my head. "I just need to get to Shannon, and the rest of them will fall."

Noose nods. "Simple."

"It's never simple." Rose reaches for Aria.

"You're not going to drop the kid, are ya? Seem kinda shaky." Noose's chin jerks back.

Rose takes an unsteady breath. "I think I'll be okay."

She grabs the kid and checks her over. She presses the baby's head against her shoulder. "I can't believe they'd hurt her."

Noose just shakes his head. The violence is coiled inside him like a cobra.

I see it. Lariat and Snare sure as fuck do.

"Can't hurt women and children when you're not breathing."

Then Rose stands on tiptoe, leaning forward and tells him something.

18

Lopez's hand on my nape is brutal and insistent. He shoves me through a door, kicking it closed behind him.

I skid to my knees, hissing through the impact. Slowly, I raise my head.

Mom is on a cot.

Her eyes are closed. I can't see her chest rise and fall with her breathing.

Is she breathing?

I struggle to a standing position, wince at the pain, and walk slowly to where Mom lies. I need to know if she's already gone.

Dreading it, I check her visually. She is breathing. But her lips are blue.

I don't know enough about medical stuff to know what happened between the time they took her and now.

There are no meds.

I sink to my haunches, devastated.

There is no tea or water.

I pick up her hand, soothing myself with the familiar motion of petting her fingers with my own. I lay my cheek against her fragile skin.

Sobs suck out of me. Mom doesn't need my tears and hysteria. She needs my strength.

Her eyes open. "Darling."

"Oh God, Mom—did they hurt you?" I wipe my eyes.

Her smile is small. "Not really. Though I don't think they were especially patient with my issues."

I dump my head on the side of her cot and cry.

Mom puts her hand on my head and strokes my hair like she used to when I was little. "I always knew I would die sooner than later, Shannon."

I lift my face, and her bulbous knuckles scrape the wet sadness that courses down my face. "Don't cry." Lying on her side, reaching up, she cradles my face with her hands. "They hope to use me as leverage to force my beautiful daughter to do ugly things."

I nod because there's no other answer.

She knows it. I know it.

Suddenly her smile turns wicked. "I dialed 9-1-1, darling. When I heard the first thug break through the door, I dialed. Then I told the wonderful girl on the other end to be quiet."

I blink. "You what?"

Slowly, she extracts my tired prepaid phone out of her lounge pants pocket.

"They didn't see this?"

She shakes her head.

I grab the phone and sit back on my butt. There are no minutes left. The battery power has one bar.

"How much?" I hit the cell on my forehead. *Think, Shannon.* "How long were you connected to 9-1-1 dispatch?"

Mom lifts one shoulder, grimaces in discomfort, and lets her arm fall softly to her side. She takes a slight breath and lets it out.

She shuts her eyes as though too tired to keep them open. "Perhaps long enough."

Her eyelids open, revealing bright eyes, armed in the fierce intelligence she's always had. "I'm dying."

I grip her hands as tightly as I dare. "No, Mom."

Noise bursts from outside the door, and we cringe.

Mom answers quietly, "Yes, Shannon. At my last doctor's appointment…well, I refused hospice."

"Oh, Mom!" I cry in a hoarse whisper, scooping her against me, but she gently pushes me away.

Searching my eyes, she says, "I thought it would be easier on you if my imminent demise occurred naturally rather than all the big build up and drama of a foretelling. Dr. Freeman did say that I needed a heart shunt.

Without one, I had days—not weeks." Her compassionate face sees only me.

I see only her.

Her fingers trail down my face. "So you see, darling, there is no extending my life. My heart is failing. But I believe I might not have failed you. There should be rescuers coming soon."

"Don't leave me, Mama," I say through my tears.

"Listen to me, Shannon. Survive this." Her eyes sharpen, glittering with her command. "Let yourself love this young, rough man."

I cock my head. "Why do you like Wring?"

She smiles. "He saved my daughter."

"Twice," I whisper.

Mom nods. "Remember what I told you when you were small?"

I do. "Actions speak louder than words."

"Yes. And his are screaming to be noticed." Her kind eyes dim. "Notice him, Shannon."

Her grip begins to soften.

"Mom!" I yell.

But her eyes are fluttering. Shutting.

Dying.

"No—no!" I grip Mom's shoulders.

Her eyes open. "I love you, darling."

"Mom…" I hug her to me, tears soaking our clothes. "I love you, too."

She blinks. Her eyes caress my face as her mouth forms a smile.

Then Mom's last breath eases out of her body.

And my will for living goes with it.

They pry my fingers from Mom, threatening to break them off. I don't need fingers to fuck, they say.

I want to die.

I'm so sad I don't know what I feel. I'm numb to everything.

Lopez hits me, and I fall.

I lie on the ground on my side and will myself to be absorbed into the hard concrete beneath me.

No one comes to save me.

"She's fucked up—that old bat of a mom dies, and she becomes a fucking corpse, too," a voice says in disgust.

"I'll get her moving."

Lopez tears off my pants. My legs flop uselessly. Fingers tear at my panties. The only other man who's touched my underwear is Wring.

"Look, man, she's crying."

"Nah," Lopez says, tugging the fragile material away from my body, "she's just leaking. All women do."

It's as though they're talking about someone else.

Rough fingers part me.

"Wow! Now this…this is a pussy."

A huge booming sound reverberates around me, shattering my numb. My autonomy.

My senses.

Chaos ensues. The pleasant roar of violence fills my ears. Flesh crushes bone.

I stare at the lights embedded in the ceiling as warm metallic rain hits my body then cools against my skin.

Something soft goes around my legs, and I sigh, finally closing my eyes. Maybe I've died, and I can be with Mom now.

I'm ready.

Then a smell of smoke and metal fills my nose.

I float.

There's no need for me to respond.

"Shannon?" a deep male voice rumbles, and beneath the layers of acrid horror, a familiar smell permeates my nose.

My lids fling open, and I suck a gasping breath then cough.

Wring.

He stands above me like a luminescent avenging angel of light and justice. His pale hair surrounds his head like a halo. Eyes like aqua gems appear to glow in the haze of the room.

Suddenly, I'm awake. I can breathe. *Feel.*

My anguished scream is caught as he lifts me, cradling me against his chest.

The soft thing I felt is wrapped around me. A blanket.

Safe, I think as my consciousness wanes to black.

19

ONE WEEK LATER

I gaze out over the foundation of my home. Lone wood two-by-fours stand like forgotten spires against the smoking remains.

Wring watches me silently, giving me space. Yet, he's closer to me than any human being could ever be.

The police did find me slightly before Wring met them at the place where Lopez conducted his business—human trafficking. Peddling flesh on the streets. Whatever he could do to directly or indirectly harm women, he was a part of it.

It didn't matter to me when I heard of his horrible childhood. Everyone has *choice*. Eventually, everyone can choose to do harm. Or not.

And Lopez chose harm every time, every day.

"You ready?" Wring asks, and I realize I've been staring off into the distance for a long time.

The clothesline is singed black, but the battered poles still stand.

"Babe," he says, wrapping an arm around my shoulder, "time to go. We don't want to be late."

I give a series of jerky nods, and he hugs me against him. I fit perfectly.

We move toward his bike. There are fourteen others lined up in the procession.

The funeral procession.

I duck my head against a cool wind that's picked up, and it lifts my simple black dress, causing the hem to hug my legs as I fight through it.

A car pulls up, and Rose exits. She holds out her hand. The girl responsible for telling Noose and Wring the one critical detail that allowed Wring to get to me.

The one detail that allowed me to have a second chance.

Wring hands me off to her, and Aria reaches for me, hooking her baby arm around my neck. Aria, Rose, and I hug. Baby smell lifts my spirits.

My new extended family huddles around me.

"Num-num," Aria whispers, pulling away.

"That kid," Rose says, shaking her head.

Everyone laughs.

"Kids got a goddamned case of worms," Noose says. But his words are said with affection, with love.

"Takes after her daddy," Rose retorts, hand on hip.

Good-natured smiles all around.

Rose takes a deep breath, squeezing my hand.
"Ready?"

I nod.

We climb into the black SUV and travel up James
Street, toward Saint James Church.

The bikers rev their engines. The rumble is like music
after the finality of Mom's death.

Another biker club showed up to pay their respects.
Chaos.

There was one especially attentive guy in their group.
Puck, I think his name was. I shake my head. He seems
so familiar somehow. Like I met him in a dream. The
guys seem to like him. Lots of back clapping and grinning going on.

I tip my head back, sucking a huge gulping inhale of
fresh air, and a rare sunbeam hits my face, warming it.

"Hey, you," Rose says, at my elbow.

I turn to face her. "You gonna be okay?"

Wring is standing with a bunch of other bikers and
happens to look up at that exact moment. His expression
says many things.

Need me? I'm here.

Are you okay?

I remember thinking when I met Wring that I
couldn't read his expressions.

Now I read them all.

I nod to Rose's question and give Wring a tentative smile. "I am now."

Rose curls an arm around my waist and tightens her hold. "I could use a friend like you."

My head eases onto her shoulder, and she presses her palm against my head.

A woman my age, with dark hair and midnight blue eyes, walks up to us. There's a really cute little girl bouncing at her side.

She looks familiar somehow, but I can't put my finger on it. *Still a little numb,* I guess.

"Hey," the brunette says with a smile, "I'm Sara—Snare's old lady."

I look at the little girl. "I'm Jaylin," she says shyly.

Sinking to my knees, I scoop my dress underneath my legs and offer her my hand.

We slowly shake hands. "It's very nice to meet you, Jaylin."

She grins, showing me a tattered bunny.

"Who's this?" I ask.

"It's Peter the Rabbit."

My eyes take in Peter, who happens to be missing an ear. "I'm very pleased to meet you as well." I shake his paw, and my hand comes away with something sticky.

I smile. Plenty of kids to adore in this group. The sentiment makes my eyes sting.

Sally fired me. Well, she didn't call it a "firing." She'd said she was sorry for my loss and the frightening circumstances surrounding it, but the library couldn't afford any more missing days from me.

I translated that to: I don't like you, and you're not getting a break.

Wring said he didn't care. He didn't give a fuck what I do. The insurance from the fire would give me some money, and I know exactly what Mom would have wanted me to do with it.

College. I think I'll be an elementary school teacher, after all.

I stand. "She looks a lot like her dad."

Sara shifts a baby to her other hip. "And what's her name?" I ask, taking a chubby hand in mine. The baby coos. Dark blue eyes blink back at me, and a tuft of inky hair stands up straight on her head. "Espie."

I frown. "What?"

Rose laughs. "It's actually Esperanza."

"That's a mouthful," I say, though it's pretty.

"*Hope* is what Espie's name means in Spanish." A sheen of tears covers Sara's eyes. "Sorry," she says, swiping at her face. "I just get all teary when I think about what I have now."

I nod stupidly because words fail me. Wring saved me—and I get what a good man means now that I've got one.

Mom's gone, and I do think that Lopez and his gang members hastened her death.

But I got to say goodbye. No one can ever take that away.

Sara smiles through her tears. "I figure Rose already told you how tight the club is?"

"Yes, but I think I got that the day I met Wring."

"Yeah, no shit," Sara says, and we laugh.

Wring strides to our little group. "Ready, babe?"

I nod.

He takes me back to the car. "The girls will get you to the cabin, and I'll follow."

He bends over me and grips my shoulder, but his lips are a feather's press against my forehead. "I'll be right behind you."

Sliding my arms around his hard waist, I cling to him for a moment. "I know," I answer quietly.

The girls and I slip into the SUV and head to Ravensdale.

"Well, your appetite sure has improved," Wring drawls.

I nod happily, shoveling in the tenth bite from the four different casseroles. "I should be grieving."

Wring kicks out his legs, lacing his hands behind his head. "Not by me, babe. You're so skinny, I say plow away." His lips twist with humor.

I set my fork down and take a deep breath. "I spent whatever extra money we had on Mom's food. Her supplements and medications. We didn't have enough…"

Suddenly, all that delicious food spread over the tiny countertop of Viper's kitchen is a big lump in my throat. Food prepared by my new family within the club. Because Mom died.

Wring leans forward, putting a large hand on my knee. "I know—I figured you were poor as shit early on. I want you to eat. I want you to eat until you puke, Shannon."

My smile is wan, and I hang my head. "I know you don't need this…complication."

Wring makes a noise of disdain deep in his throat. "Fuck that. There's not one of us guys—well, I guess Lariat—who doesn't seem to be a damn magnet for complicated women." He chuckles.

I can't help my smile. Rose and Sara had filled me in on their transition from "citizens" to biker brides.

"You're not a 'complication,' Shannon." Wring pulls me onto his lap. "You're the woman I love."

I lift my chin. I gulp, afraid to hope.

His hand cradles my jaw. "I didn't save you."

I open my mouth to protest, and his fingers press against my lips. "You saved me. I was this scooped-out husk. Couldn't sleep. Didn't give any fucks. Got outta the service, estranged from what little family I had, decided to stick with the one I knew."

"Noose and Lariat?" I say, thinking they'd all been in the war together. Wring and I had done more than just make love since that day my house burned down.

We'd communicated. Connected.

I didn't think I could be truly intimate with another human being again.

But I was wrong. I could. *I am.*

Mom's loss is a sucking void, but Wring is the salve to a wound I didn't think would heal.

"Snare, too," he adds, brushing a stray hair from my face and tucking it behind my ear. Wring's stubble tickles my face as he whispers against my temple, "I got something to show you."

I lean away, studying his face, a flutter in my stomach.

"Don't give me that look. It's a good thing. No more awful for you, Shannon. It's all good from here on out."

I wrap my arms around his neck. I feel safe.

Loved.

20

WRING

Her warm back is pressed tightly against mine. I cover her wrapped arms with my hand, easily steering my bike up the winding hill toward my new place.

Shannon probably doesn't remember I was having a house built on the property adjacent to Snare's.

I try not to let the tension sing through my body, but it's a hard trick.

I've fought for my life and for others, but the possibility of Shannon's rejection looms large.

This girl holds my gonads—and my heart—in her delicate hands. With the wrong answer, she could crush me.

I don't have it in me to go back to that voided-out existence where I just shit, eat, and fuck with insomnia and nightmares.

Shannon's put an end to my misery and given me something to believe in besides surviving.

I come to a stop in front of the place and kill the engine.

I'm not a visionary, but I vaguely remember my grandparent's house. It was a solid old farmhouse with a couple of dormer windows above and an expansive front porch.

Using that as a model, I choose a Terhune house plan called "the Hannibal."

A square copula graces the top of the attached garage, which doesn't face the front of the circular gravel drive like the ones on a lot of modern houses. The doors load from the side, so it's all picturesque house from the front.

Didn't want to copy Snare too much, so the paint's on hold. Just painted with a pure clean white primer at the moment.

Shannon slides off the quiet bike and stands there, staring at the house.

God—*what if she hates it?*

"Is this your house, Wring?"

I stay quiet.

Shannon looks at me over her shoulder, her beautiful clear pale-emerald eyes wide.

I nod. "It's the one I said I was getting built."

"It's beautiful," she breathes then ducks her face away from my eyes.

"Hey."

Shannon looks up.

"It can be your house, too."

She shakes her head. "I don't want to be a pity case. I've already relied on you too much. I—"

"No."

Her eyes meet mine.

"I'm a deliberate dude. I don't fucking take sweet butts out to my digs and give 'em a tour, Shannon."

My hands fist. "I don't go to club whore's mom's funeral."

I pull her to me, widening my legs, and her small body moves between them. "I don't love anyone, Shannon."

Tears begin to run down her face.

I wipe them away with the pads of my thumbs. "I love you."

She nods, smiling.

Why do chicks cry when they're not sad?

Then she gives me the answer I'm looking for. The only one that matters.

"I love you, too, Wring."

My chest swells into a tight knot. "Hoping you'd say that." I take her hand and tow her inside the house.

I run a finger over the countertop. It's some kind of cold stone, swirly patterns of deep charcoal gray and creamy white look like spilt glitter stirred together into a delicious pattern.

"House isn't painted yet," Wring says from behind me.

I lift an eyebrow. "Oh, I thought white was it."

He shakes his head gently. "Nah. Looking for a woman's touch. One woman. One touch."

He takes my hand and puts it on his healthy erection.

I blush. The man's insatiable.

Thank God for lust, because I think it's all that saved me from my grief. That, and Mom's blessing. She seemed to like Wring from the moment she set eyes on him.

"We're gonna christen the place." He leads me to a bed. It's flat on the middle of a living room floor, the only furniture in the place.

On the center there's a small box.

Blue velvet.

I cover my mouth. I've only known Wring a little over two weeks. Blinking back tears, I drop his hand and slowly walk toward the small navy speck in the sea of crisp white bed linen.

"Wring—"

"Nope. Open it, Shannon."

I lower myself to the bed. My fingers shake as I grab the box. I don't open it right away. The soft plush of the velvet warms inside my fingers.

Finally, I crack the lid.

"You didn't have a dad to ask," Wring explains as I stare at the ring.

Neither of us says anything about my mom.

"And I don't know anything about jewelry for chicks." He gives a rough scrub of his short blond hair with a palm. "So, I saw my mother. Finally."

I look up at him.

His neck reddens, and he swipes a hand over his nape. "Anyways, she said I could have my grandmother's ring when I asked." Wring looks away, and I see his nervousness.

I don't say anything. I *can't*. My heart's so full, I feel like I'm drowning.

In the best way imaginable.

"If you don't"—he shrugs—"like it, I can get you something else…"

I stand and go to him. Hugging him around his narrow waist, I splay my fingers over the muscles of his lower back. "I love it."

His shoulders sag in apparent relief. "I know this is fast, Shannon." He tilts my chin back. "But you feel right." He grabs my hand and puts it against his heart. "Here." His eyes hood. "Let's get hitched."

I start crying again.

He crouches down so his face is level with mine. "I'm going to take a leap and guess all these tears mean yes."

I give an emphatic nod, too emotionally beaten to verbalize my consent.

But my answer is a thousand times yes.

He plucks the box from my fingers and takes out the slim platinum band encrusted with diamonds on its circumference. Slivers of carved half-moons hold the large center diamond. It's old-fashioned. Unique.

Like Wring. Like us.

He slips the ring on the ring finger of my left hand. It fits perfectly.

He chuckles softly. "Fits awesome. Grandma was tiny, too." Wring kisses my forehead.

"What were you saying about christening?" I ask, my grin sly.

"House isn't gonna feel like it's mine until I have you in it, under me."

I fall backward on the bed as the sunlight catches the facets of the diamonds, casting them far and wide like chipped rainbows.

Shannon spreads herself beneath me, and I make short work of my clothes.

I only take time to carefully fold my cut and put it on the countertop. The rest of my shit gets dumped on the floor.

Mattress is the only piece of furniture I have in the whole place.

Shannon's all I need, and now I've made her mine.

Striding back over to her naked body, I kneel between her legs.

Conveniently, Shannon shed her clothes. They lie on top of my own.

I spread her creamy thighs with the flat of my palms, taking in the gorgeous pink sight of her pussy.

Hot as fuck.

"You always look at me." A self-conscious shadow lingers in her voice.

"I'm a worshiper," I say softly, running a finger down her glistening folds.

"Worshiper?" She quirks an eyebrow, but there's a flush to her skin, a depth to her one-word question.

"Yeah, one of those dudes that wants to get down on his hands and knees for pussy."

She frowns, clearly taking my words the wrong way. Talking isn't my best thing.

"But I never felt like I did much of it until I saw yours." I put my hand over her mound and sweep the tip of my thumb inside her wetness.

We groan together.

"Yeah," I say softly, kicking my head back. "It's all about your pussy, Shannon."

Her blush is a brushfire of red over her fair skin. "You talk dirty."

"You like it," I say, thinking about her coming against my face while I talked about my tongue fucking her cunt.

She really liked it then, pulsing around me while I stabbed it inside her deep.

"Yeah, I do."

"Besides…" I meet her beautiful green eyes. "Now I'm making you legit."

I hike her hips up and place the barest bit of me inside her, stroking into her about a third of the way. Gets her off fast. Chicks are sensitive that first third.

My thumb begins to work her clit hard. I keep stroking in shallow thrusts.

Shannon's so fucking tight, I have to think about doing dirty laundry to keep from coming.

Then she hooks her heels behind my back, and I groan, biting my lip hard, tasting blood.

"Shannon," I grit out with hard-won restraint.

"Ah!" she yells softly, tossing her arms behind her head. Her mouth parts, and she begins to pant, moving her body back and forward with the thrusts of my dick.

I shove my length in all the way, the end of me at the end of her.

We throb together for a suspended moment.

"I'm coming," she says softly. Her legs spread slightly wider, and I withdraw then thrust again.

Shannon's pussy pulses around me, clenching my cock tight enough that I can hardly breathe.

With a final thrust, I bury myself to the hilt, bathing her insides with everything I have.

Everything I am.

I grab her wrists and lay myself on top of her, stabbing my elbows at either side of her head. I kiss every inch of her face, leaving her mouth for last.

I pull back and chuckle at the dazed expression in her eyes. "Hmm…" Kiss, suck, peck. "You seem satisfied."

Her soft expression causes me physical pain—it's that powerful. To see that love she's got for me shining from her eyes.

"I think I blew a circuit or something." Shannon sighs in total contentment.

I roll off her and tuck her in beside my body, tossing a leg over hers. "Nope, electrical's good."

She wraps her fingers around my cock and squeezes me softly.

I hiss in a breath.

"So good." She kisses me back.

We don't get out of the makeshift bed for the rest of the day.

EPILOGUE
One year later

I toss my books in the back of my VW Rabbit and slide behind the wheel.

The late summer sun slants through the windshield, momentarily blinding me. My wedding rings twinkle back at me.

My smile is its own light. A lot has happened in the last year.

Miracles. Love. Loss.

And most importantly—hope.

Wring takes me there.

I should go to Mom's graveside on her birthday each year. Celebrate her life instead of the day she died. But that's not how life works.

I'm marking when mine began.

Mom released me. She gave me advice, which I took. She left earlier than I wanted, but somehow, in a way, she gave me Wring.

Wring hangs out against a tree, knee bent and biker's boot planted against the deeply furrowed bark. His hooded eyes watch me, constantly scanning the area.

He takes my protection seriously.

There's no reason to worry, though. The Bloods disbanded after their leader was killed and cops were crawling all over their turf.

Wring still worries. I think it's just in his nature. And Noose's and Snare's. The jury's out on Lariat. Maybe there's no woman to be his other half.

Arranging the flowers at Mom's gravestone, I talk to her. "I did it, Mom. I believed. I trusted."

The diamonds inside my wedding set sparkle as I spread the petals perfectly at the base of the granite marker.

A fat tear drops on my hand.

Then another.

I wish Mom could have been there to meet Wring's mom and the guys—even Viper. That thought makes me smile.

But she directed me toward the man who's now my husband. He didn't tell me until after we were married that he'd spoken to her before she was taken.

Wring told her he would always protect me. No matter what.

Mom believed him.

I'd wondered how she could have died so peacefully, in a building full of gangbangers who'd done everything but steal our property. I know now that it was because I was her greatest possession. Not our house.

Me.

That's what I finally realized: Mom loved people above things.

I turn and look at Wring.

He straightens from his perch against the trunk. "Ready, babe?"

I nod then giggle, shooting my arm straight up in the air. "A little help?" I wink at him.

He saunters over.

"And to think that I was forcing you to eat." He gently pulls me to a standing position, and I put a hand to my aching lower back.

He puts his hand on my swollen belly.

"Love that I knocked ya up."

I smirk. "I think you liked the process."

"That, too, babe." Wring bends over me, kissing me thoroughly over Mom's grave.

I have to think she's up in heaven, smiling down on her daughter and unborn grandchild.

I finally found my slice of heaven, right here on earth.

THE END

Thank you for your attention:

Marata Eros is the pen name for **Tamara Rose Blodgett**, *a bestselling dark fantasy writer.*

Love **ROAD KILL MC?** *Please read on for a sample of another Marata Eros work…*

DEATH WHISPERS

A DEATH SERIES NOVEL

BOOK 1

New York Times Bestselling Author
TAMARA ROSE BLODGETT

1

Pre-Biology sucked, but the subject was mandatory in eighth grade. I walked in and slumped into my seat. We were going to be dissecting frogs, and I wasn't excited about it.

John sat down next to me with two pencils up his nose.

"Hey, Caleb."

"Hey. Did ya make sure the erasers were in there first?" I asked him.

"Yeah, duh." The pencils bounced as he spoke. For a smart guy, he had some weird ideas about self-entertainment.

"You still buzzing?" he asked.

"Yeah, it's on and off." I felt kind of defensive about that and didn't really want to talk about it.

"I've been thinking about that," he said.

I wondered briefly how he could think with pencils up his nose. A mystery. "Yeah?"

"I think you have the undead creeper, like that Parker dude," John said.

That would be bad. "He's the one that could corpse-raise, right?" I asked.

I had just been thinking about how much that ability sucked. However, the rareness of corpse-raising might come in handy. But that being my ability wasn't likely. Mr. Collins went to the whiteboard and started to explain how to pin down the frogs.

"Government took him. Bye-bye…gone." John made a fluttering motion with his hand like a bird flying away. The pencils kept bouncing in a distracting way.

I'd heard about that. Corpse manipulation was rare. Jeffrey Parker was the only recorded case.

"Are you shitting me? Why do you think? Dead people? Come on." I got an image of zombies with M-60s. I was interested for a change. Sometimes John would lose me in a tech rant, and it was all over.

"No, think about it. They could get people raised and force them to do stuff. From a distance, they'd look like they were alive, important people." He raised his eyebrows.

"Presidents?"

"Rulers or whoever," John said. "He was a five-point. He could do the whole tamale. I think the government exploits whatever they can; using whoever they can."

I laughed.

"What?" he asked.

"I can't take you seriously. You look like a dumb-ass." The pencils dangled indignantly inside each nostril, humiliated.

John pulled them out, checking the ends for gold.

I'd been wondering why my head was buzzing. I tried to remember when the it'd started. I had no idea what triggered it. I wondered if John could be right?

"Okay, people," Collins said. "Zip up here and pick up your trays. Your sterilized utensils should already be at your desks."

John went for our trays, minus the attractive pencils. I stared out the window, the rain rivulets that looked like gray streamers marring the glass.

I shook my head, clearing fuzziness. I couldn't get rid of the buzzing, a dull noise that ebbed and flowed. As soon as I had entered the classroom, it had increased. It was starting to sound like people whispering.

"Here. One frog for the both of us." John plunked down a frog that had once been green but was now a bone-gray. The pins staking it to the board gleamed under the LEDs.

Suddenly, I felt as though the earth was swiveling on its axis with me at the top. The whispering grew in volume then images of a marsh flooded my head. A frog, in the bloom of its life, shiny with amphibian iridescence, leapt to a log, hoping to fool a water moccasin.

Right behind you! I shouted.

But the frog didn't seem to hear me.

A motor boat was closing in on the frog. A man leaned out, getting ready to take capture the frog with a loose net on the end of a long metal pole. I heard the frog's thoughts: Strange predator. Must seek cover… noise…hurts…

No! No!

More visions came. With every cut my classmates made, I saw stuff from other frogs' lives. I realized through some dim sense that I was lying on the floor. I think I might have passed out for a few minutes.

"He bit it over a frog? Seriously?" Carson yelled.

Brett, not to be outdone, caterwauled, "He's a total girl!"

Collins was moving his hand in front of my face, holding up fingers, but I was caught in the grip of the death memories absorbing my consciousness. My vision grayed at the edges. A pin point of black expanded in the center, and I knew no more.

Trees surrounding the cemetery danced in the languid breeze of the mild spring night. Headstones glimmered like loose teeth, and the whispering was like a steady thrumming of white noise in my head. My hands grew clammy.

I looked behind me at my two friends who'd come to support me. They had discovered my secret: that I could hear the dead. Proving to Carson and Brett that I had Affinity for the Dead—or AFTD—wouldn't keep them off my back completely, but it'd notch down their stupid to something me and my posse could manage.

"Caleb, show them you're not a frickin' poser," Jonesy said.

"I don't pose."

I took a step through the Victorian-style gate, my foot touching its reluctant toe on hallowed ground.

The feeling of being forced pressed uncomfortably against my mind.

As I crossed the threshold, the whispering turning into voices. One whispered stronger than the others. As if an invisible string pulled me along, I was drawn toward one of the gravestones. The marker stood sentinel near the middle of the cemetery, glowing softly in the moonlight. I stopped in front of it.

"Clyde Thomas, born 1900, died 1929."

"Wake me…" someone whispered.

"What?" I asked.

"Wake me…"

"Caleb, who are you talking to?" John asked.

I swung my head in slow-motion, as if moving it through quicksand. Blood rushed in my ears, and my heart beat thick and heavy in my chest. Everything became crystallized in that moment. John's frizzy hair and freckles stood out like measles. A microscopic chip lay like an imperfect shadow on the headstone, a shining stark contrast to the white marble.

Something…something…was building, rising up as if underwater and rushing to the surface. I was supposed to finalize something, but what? John's mouth was moving but no sound was coming out. He was arguing with Jonesy and flailing his arms as he spoke. The whispering of the corpse in the earth was so loud it drowned out his words.

Jonesy's hand suddenly connected with my face. My teeth slammed into my tongue, and the taste of copper pennies filled my mouth. I leaned over, and a drop of blood hung tremulously on my bottom lip, before falling to the grave like a black gem.

Everything clicked into place, vertigo spinning the graveyard on its side as if it had been waiting for that moment. The ground rushed toward my face, and I threw out my hands to brace my fall. My fingers bit into the damp earth. A hand broke through the ground like a spear through flesh and grasped my wrist. The vise-like grip and intense coldness of the grave lingering on its dead flesh made my breath catch in my throat.

The head of the corpse broke free of the ground, then the hand released me. I scooted backward and got to my feet, swaying, overcome with some unidentifiable emotion. I had done it, but I didn't know how to undo it.

The corpse moved toward me with purpose, using the undisturbed ground for leverage. When it reached my feet, another drop of my blood landed with a dull plop on the corpse's forehead. Jonesy ran out of the cemetery and stood at a "safe" range from what the ground had disgorged.

The zombie's gaze fixed on me. It put a hand on its knee and began to push itself upright. Dull, lank strands of hair hung loosely from a scalp of rotten sinew. "Why have you awoken me?" The words sounded garbled.

I stared at it. "You asked me to."

John was standing at my right, trying to mask a fine, all-over tremble. His freckles stood out from his pale face like beacons of fright.

"What the hell is this?"

I turned and gave him a duh look.

The zombie's eyes rolled wetly in their sockets.

"Why have you awoken me?" it repeated, shambling a little closer.

The smell...wow. It rose like a torrent of rotting garbage. John clapped his hand over his nose and backed up a bit.

The corpse took another step closer to me.

"Got any brilliant suggestions?" I asked John, keeping my eyes on the zombie.

"Sorry. I don't have the Zombie Handbook handy," John said.

Not helpful.

The corpse tilted its head. "You're just a boy. For what purpose have you disturbed my slumber?"

"I, um…I didn't…uh, mean to…um, wake you up." I wasn't usually so tongue-tied, but meeting a corpse in the flesh—ha, ha—seemed to have stolen my ability to speak coherently.

"You do not know what you would have of me? You use your life-force to awaken me and without purpose? Put me back." His clothes hung in tatters, and the smell was definitely old, dark coffin, not that I knew what that smelled like.

John's look clearly said, Do something! What I hadn't told my friends was that I had never thought that I could actually raise the dead. But there the dead guy was, standing before me in all his rotting glory.

"To whom much is given, much is expected. Put me back," he said.

Adults were all the same, even dead ones; lecture, lecture.

"How?" I asked.

"You are the necromancer, boy, not I."

"I'm a what?" I felt surprisingly calm. For the first time, there were no whispers. Perfect, blessed silence filled my head. Talking to the dead seemed like the most natural thing in the world. I could still taste the blood from my busted lip. Its eyeballs were inky marbles staring back with uncanny devotion.

"A necromancer. A diviner of the black arts," he replied.

I thought about that for a minute. Things had only gotten über-weird when Jonesy had smacked me. I looked back at the corpse, no longer feeling that sense of swimming power just beneath the surface. I needed to regain that essence—fast.

"Ah…hang on a minute," I told the corpse. I turned to John.

"John, give me your blade."

"What the heck, Caleb? What are you planning to do with that"—John pointed at the patient corpse, "… thing?" Who was as immobile out of his grave as in.

"I figure my blood made it jump out of its grave, so now I need some to put him back. And you're going to help me."

John's face got even paler. "Ah, we're good friends and all, but no, not a good plan! We don't know that for sure anyway."

John needed to ante up the blood, or it was going to be a long night. I tapped my foot on the disturbed mess of the grave. "Here's the deal. Let's do a little 'friendship blood bank' just for the sake of putting the dead guy back in his grave, eh? Just give me your arm."

John took a deep breath. "Okay, but you're going to owe me big time." He held out his arm.

I placed the blade on his forearm then made a thin slit in the skin. John let out a little gasp. When crimson oozed out, I repeated the process with my own arm then pressed my arm against John's.

A vibrating tuning fork of trembling power welled up inside my body. A strange mixture of fear, dread and excitement paralyzed me. My teeth throbbed with the intensity of it. The zombie's hand snaked out and curled around my arm. Its skin felt cold against my warm flesh, like iced tentacles. I swabbed a blot of blood with the fingers of my other hand and dabbed it on the zombie's forehead like war paint.

The dead guy rolled those empty eyes up at me, its dead bones clinging to my fingertips.

We shared a suspended moment in time, a terrible beauty of precariously balanced control.

"Go back and rest," I said, feeling that I was choosing for both of us.

The zombie reluctantly let go of my arm, sand through a sieve, then lay down on the disturbed ground. His grave encased him in a shroud of earth.

John and I stared at each other over the grave for a swollen minute, his face showing a mixture of sympathy and dread. I was a corpse-raiser—one of only two in existence—and that was not a safe thing to be. John knew what that would mean for me in the world we lived in.

I was shaking from the intensity of the experience and thoughts of the future. This was not the same as Biology experiments and roadkill, this was real, huge. Looking outside the cemetery perimeter at two enemies and one friend, I knew it was time to swear the group to secrecy. A trickle of sweat slithered down my back and pooled at the waistband of my jeans, instantly chilling my fevered skin. I didn't want the same future as Parker. That loss of freedom was so not a part of my plan.

John and I headed out of the cemetery in a wave of uncertain promise.

2

I smacked my alarm. Just five more minutes, I thought, dozing off.

"Caleb!" Mom yelled from downstairs.

I sat up. "Yeah?"

"School!"

I stumbled out of my bed and looked at the clothes on the floor. Hmm, what to wear that wasn't too wrinkled.

I picked up a pair of jeans and a shirt and took an experimental whiff. Good enough. I jerked on the jeans with a hop and a zip. I opened my sock drawer—a couple of socks, not matched but clean. Happy day.

I trudged downstairs to the kitchen. I sat at the table. "You cookin' today?" I asked, hopeful.

"No, but you're eating."

Eating in the morning blows. I was that lazy. I'd open the fridge, nothing. Then the freezer, repeat. I usually ended up cramming a yogurt down.

She opened the fridge. "What flavor?"

"Do we have blueberry?" That was the only non-barf fruit I could think about eating that early.

She handed me the yogurt container. "Last one."

"Where's Dad?"

"He is working on that new project."

Great. Hopefully not anything new for kids to rant about. Mom and Dad were on the opposite end of the spectrum. She was free-spirited and thought the mystery of life and choice were taken away when the puzzle of the genome mapping was solved. Since my dad was an integral part of the team who achieved that accomplishment, we had an interesting family life.

"Does that mean he'll be home for supper tonight? I've got something to talk to him about." I wisely didn't mention the whole corpse-raising episode. Dad was logic and fairness mixed. He'd know what to do. This…I might need some help on.

"Yes, he will, you know how important meal time is," Mom said.

Maybe, maybe not. Science was important to Dad.

After I wolfed down the yogurt, I made a two-point shot at the trash can. Swish! No mess, but that didn't stop the frown from forming on Mom's face.

I moved quickly to grab my backpack, but she blocked my way, and I was forced to look up at her. Every girl in the world was taller than I was, even my own mother.

She brushed the hair out of my eyes, but it immediately flopped back down. "You need a haircut."

"No, Mom." A time sucker was all a haircut was, and I had more important things to do.

I slung my pack over my shoulder and left. I wanted to reconnoiter with the dudes, get things straight in my head from last night. Once outside, I slowed to a walk. I'd still be there early, and I was feeling lazy.

The canopy of trees allowed the morning light to filter through, speckling the ground with sunspots. My head began the familiar thrumming, a buzz seeping into the crevices of my mind as I walked toward the school.

I stopped. The buzzing became whispering. My heart rate sped up, my breath quickened, and my palms dampened.

The voices of the dead had arrived.

The whispering grew louder. The dull roar of the insidious voices was like a magnet, pulling me toward the forest. I followed it and was rewarded with even higher volume.

At the edge of the tree line, a crumpled body, lay beside a ditch. The head was canted at an awkward angle. My hands trembled as the whispering gave way to images flooding my head like a pulse-screen.

Headlights burst like twin spots before the cat's eyes as she tried to escape them. Rushing forward, she sprinted across the street. She didn't time the advance properly, and the twin orbs bore down on her.

Pain. Intense pain and blinding light.

The cat thought of her litter, her people…then, she was no more.

My breath returned in a paralyzing rush. I stood next to her small body. She had shared the last moments of her life with me.

I remained there, taking it in and realizing that life as I knew it was never going to be the same. I wasn't going to breeze through being a teenager.

Snapping back to reality I realized I was the Pied Piper of road kill.

Great. Definitely my life-goal.

I thought of the frogs in biology. There had been so many that I hadn't been able to camouflage what happened to me.

I wished I could develop something righteous like pyrokinesis. That would be tight. At least only Brett and Carson knew the corpse-raising part. Getting them to cooperate with silence was another deal. People were going to get suspicious.

I trudged toward school, my limbs heavy and my head swimming with the heaviness of an undead moment. I lifted my hands. The fine shaking was almost gone. I wiped the sweat off my face with the back of my hand. I needed to get a hold of myself. I was on it.

The familiar doors to my daily prison came into view. I walked the rest of the way with my head down and went inside the school. I spotted the "cemetery group" right away.

John and Jonesy stood apart from the others. Almost five-ten with a shock of frizzy, carrot-colored hair and pale blue eyes, John looked a little freakish, but he was my main dude, my go-to guy when things went sideways. In stark contrast, Jonesy had short, nappy hair and teeth that stood out like white Chiclets in his dark face. He was taller than I was, but built stocky. They'd been my friends since kindergarten.

Standing a few feet away from my friends was the rest of the group. They were a mixed bag, didn't feel solid. It would take some clever conniving to get promises of secrecy from the rest. Brett Mason and Carson Hamilton. They had identical white-blond hair and were about the same height, making them hard to tell apart. They'd been in my class since kindergarten too, but not in a good way.

Edging through the throng of kids, I made my way to John and Jonesy. Jonesy leaned against the locker, arms crossed. John seemed ready to explode, not a typical look for him.

Jonesy nodded at me. "Sorry about the bludgeoning."

"Yeah…what the hell?" I asked.

"Your face sorta got in the way."

"Oh…really?" Gee, hadn't noticed that.

"It was an accident, John and I were discussing—"

John broke in. "Arguing."

Jonesy glared at him. "I changed my mind is all."

I raised my eyebrows, Jonesy never switched gears.

"About the merit of them knowing," John finished.

I glanced at Bret and Carson. Too late. The milk was spilled and dripping on the floor. They walked over to us.

"I wasn't pulling a hypo in Biology," I told them, "and now Aptitude Testing is coming up."

Brett smirked. "Yeah. You have your dad to thank for that."

I caught sight of a grape-sized bruise the color of pale chartreuse at the base of Brett's neck. His smirk faded as he shifted his shoulder to make his shirt cover the mark.

Jonesy straightened. "Shut up. It's Caleb's ass on the line." He jabbed his thumb at my chest. "You know what happens when you hit the radar as a corpse raiser. He'd be a government squirrel, like that Parker dude."

"Nobody wants to have their life planned by somebody else," John said.

"My dad didn't have anything to do with that," I pointed out.

"But thanks to him, everyone's tested now because of the mapping. All the do-gooders want to 'realize our full potential.'" Brett made air quotes as he said the last phrase. "What an ass-load of crap that was."

Carson nodded. "So even if we don't want to be mathematicians or scientists, we're on that freight train until it reaches the depot."

His murky-green eyes burrowed into mine.

It was an old argument. Kinda like being the preacher's kid, I got blamed for everything my dad did…or didn't do.

"You dickface…" Jonesy pointed at Carson. "Yeah you. It isn't Caleb's fault that his dad started that ball rolling with the mapping. If it hadn't been him, it would've been someone else."

Carson clenched his hands into fists and looked as though he might take a swing at Jonesy. He didn't like being told the obvious. Probably shouldn't have opened his mouth and crammed a foot in there until he choked. Kinda brain dead—kinda consistent.

"Listen, guys," I said. "This isn't helping. It's the now we need to figure out. I don't want to pop a five-point AFTD on the APs. They're only a week away? My dad"— I saw Carson roll his eyes, but I ignored him—"says that puberty is when they test because scientists have proven that abilities come on then, sometimes for the first time." Not for me, I added silently.

The first bell gave its shrill beckon. I looked at Brett and Carson. "I need you guys to cover for me. At least until after the testing."

"You can't force us, Hart," Brett said.

Carson nodded. "Yeah, just because Daddy's famous doesn't give you clout."

So much for that.

"How about doing it because it's the right thing to do?" Jonesy asked.

"Because it's the human thing to do," John interjected.

"He's not human." Carson said, stabbing a finger toward my chest.

"You got that right," Brett agreed.

They turned and moved into the multicolor sea of kids.

"Did ya see that bruise necklace Brett was wearing?" I asked.

"It's the dad," John answered.

Jonesy turned his liquid eyes to me. "Feel sorry for him, Caleb? Don't go soft on me, bro. You're always giving jackasses the benefit of the doubt."

My conscious teetered on the balance of right and wrong. Brett had it bad, but he chose to act the way he did.

Jonesy clapped me on the back "Yeah, my cup of care is empty too."

3

The Js and I went to shop class. I was making my mom a heart-shaped box, though my heart was definitely not in it.

After talking to the ass-monkeys, I couldn't get the genome out of my head.

The mapping of 2010 happened under pressure from President O'Llama. Desperate for health care reform, the government wanted to activate "markers" for the population. Mapping the human genome was the key to identifying potential for cancer, heart disease, stroke, and even alcoholism and drug addictions. If the people wanted government health care, they would have to be mapped, and have a microchip implanted that contained their genetic codes. Refusal of the microchip meant no health care. The program had been expanded, and disease markers weren't the only things on those chips.

The teacher, Mr. Morginstern, approached our table with a cheery "Good morning, fellas!"

It was criminal that he was so happy. Didn't he know the Monday-is-hateful-rule?

"Hey," I mumbled, as Jonesy and John gave Morginstern the nod.

Morginstern was excited about teaching and we were excited about…school ending for the day.

"So how was your weekend? Do anything interesting?"

Yeah.

I imagined a conversation like: Ah no problem, Mr. Morginstern, just creeping around illegally in a grave-yard, raising a corpse, enemies seeing the blow-by-blow… real interesting.

Instead, I shrugged and said, "It was okay."

Jonesy looked to be choking back a laugh. I gave him a don't-blow-it look.

John was unflappably silent as usual, controlling a sly grin with effort, the anchor to our madness.

Morginstern seemed to accept our weird responses, and he went over the whole process of our boxes again. Adults were painfully redundant.

We got to decide what kind of box to make. Heart shaped was the hardest, but I was a masochist. I got out my sandpaper—one-twenty grit, extra fine.

A fine dust fell from the interior arc of the heart onto the work table. The sanding from the three of us served as an excellent conversation concealer.

John whispered, "So what's the plan?"

"I don't know yet," I replied. "I gotta think about it more. I'm not ending up like Parker."

"Ask your dad," Jonesy said. "He's the genius."

"Quiet, smack attack."

Jonesy ducked his head. "I'm sorry, bro."

I grinned. "Gotcha. Just wanted to see what you'd say."

"Oh man! Don't do that, dude!" Jonesy threw his sandpaper at me.

I deflected it with my arm, and the paper landed on John, getting embedded in his hair.

Morginstern gave us a warning glare. "Caleb Hart! Jonesy, John, no throwing supplies."

"Stop screwing around," John hissed. "This is serious."

As serious as a heart attack. I struggled not to laugh. "I'll talk with my dad tonight. He'll have ideas."

"He's got resources, right?" Jonesy asked.

I smiled. "Using your big-boy words Jonesy?"

We all laughed and agreed to meet up at my place.

I had every class with John except PE. Jonesy was in my PE class, though. I was never without a J. Jonesy and I liked PE because we got to check out the girls. There was one in particular that I liked a lot.

When we got to the gym, Jonesy said, "I want to play dodge ball today."

"Yeah, that'll happen. 'No head shots, no body shots above the waist, no leg shots.'" I said, imitating Miss Griswold's annoying voice.

I sighed. Dodge ball rocked, but Griswold was a joy sucker.

Then Jade LeClerc walked by. I tracked her with my eyes. Her jet-black hair gleamed like a curtain of silk waiting to be touched. She had the greatest eyes, green like a cat's. A memory shimmered just out of reach—a red shirt, concrete, and dirt.

Jonesy gave me a strategic elbow to the side, and the image slipped away like a vapor.

"Ow!" I turned to him. "What was that for?"

"Stop staring," Jonesy said. "Why do you like her anyway? She's kinda emo."

"No she's not, she just wants people to think she is. Keeps them away," I said, trying to recapture that fleeting shard of the past.

"Oh, and you're such a girl expert. Right!" Jonesy laughed.

I scowled at him. "I've watched her. She doesn't make a move to be anyone's friend, but there's something cool about her."

"She's too weird. Pick someone else. Look at them all." He spread his arms to include the bounty of girls.

My eyes strayed back to Jade. She just looked unique. "I'm gonna talk to her."

"You've had English and pre-Biology with her, what, almost two semesters? We're in fourth quarter, and you still haven't said anything. Besides, what's she gonna think when she finds out about what you can do? She saw you pass out, right?"

I couldn't deny his reasoning there. Who hadn't seen me bite it? Maybe once I had a plan on how to hide what I was, I could say hey.

"Maybe she doesn't need to ever know."

Jonesy arched one eyebrow, the whites of his eyes wider in his brown face. "You can't cover forever, bro." He shrugged.

I figured, but I liked to fantasize.

Miss Griswold blew her whistle, and we lined up for warm-ups. We were in alphabetical order, so Jonesy wasn't close to me, and neither was Jade. But I was next to Carson Hamilton.

"Hey, Hart. Thinking about any ghosts?"

Carson-the-Clever. Yeah, right.

I ignored him and started doing jumping jacks with the others. "Switch drill!" Griswold shrieked.

We went down to our knees for push-ups.

I finally responded, "Don't be a tard, Carson. You and Brett said that I was faking shit. I wasn't. I proved I'm AFTD." I huffed out five more.

"Switch drill!" Griswold's irritating voice rallied for the final insult.

We stood up for jumping power lunges. I hated those. I put out one foot and lunged so my knee didn't pass my toe then, up, jump, other side. Talking was almost impossible.

Carson managed. He had a lot of hot air.

"AFTD is so rare only freaks have it. That's why they took Parker away. The military wanted to quarantine his ass to protect everyone else."

Carson dropping another pearl of wisdom. Like I care.

Hop. Switch legs.

"Stop!" Griswold yelled.

Panting, I turned to Carson. "Nobody'll believe you. You didn't believe until the cemetery." He'd look like an idiot if he told people I was a corpse raiser (like we were running around in droves). Carson was all about image.

He looked thoughtful; Carson was a rock with lips.

"Maybe I won't tell anybody, but me and Brett might want something."

He looked down at me and smirked.

We glared at each other until Griswold waddled over to stand in front of us. I wondered how teachers always seemed to know just when something was going down.

Griswold put her hands on her considerable hips. "Problem here, boys?"

"No problem, Miss Griswold," Carson said.

I said the obligatory, "No, Miss Griswold."

Just as she moved out of hearing range, Carson said, "Hag."

Griswold turned around and yelled, "Time for dodge ball! Pick your teams."

The guys gave a collective groan, and the girls didn't look any happier. At least I got to look at Jade, the high-light of PE.

Jonesy gave me a questioning look from across the gym, Carson and Brett were fast moving from irritating to becoming a problem—one that I planned to contain, creatively.

Jonesy would scheme, John would deliberate and I would definitely do.

<u>Also available in paperback</u>

Volumes 1-3 **FREE** *for a limited time!*

ACKNOWLEDGMENTS

I published **The Druid** and **Death Series** in 2011 with the encouragement of my husband, and continued because of you, my Reader. Your faithfulness through comments, suggestions, spreading the word and ultimately purchasing my work with your hard-earned money gave me the incentive, means and inspiration to continue.

There are no words that are sufficiently adequate to express my thankfulness for your support. But know this: TDS novellas continued past HARVEST only because of you.

I truly feel connected to my readers. It is obvious to me, but I'll say the words anyway for clarity: a written work is just words on pages if they are not read by my readers. As I write this I get a lump in my throat; your enjoyment of my work affects me that deeply.

You guys are the greatest, each and every one of ya-

Marata (Tamara) xo

Special Thanks:
You, my reader.
Hubs, who is my biggest fan.
Cameren, without whom, there would be no books.

ABOUT THE AUTHOR

Tamara Rose Blodgett: happily married mother of four sons. Dark fiction writer. Reader. Dreamer. Home restoration slave. Tie dye zealot. Coffee addict. Bead Slut. Digs music.

She is also the *New York Times* Bestselling author of *A Terrible Love,* written under the pen name, **Marata Eros,** and over ninety-five other titles, to include the #1 international bestselling erotic Interracial/African-American **TOKEN** serial and her #1 Amazon bestselling Dark Fantasy novel, *Death Whispers.* Tamara writes a variety of dark fiction in the genres of erotica, fantasy, horror, romance, sci-fi and suspense. She lives in the midwest with her family and pair of disrespectful dogs.

Connect with Tamara:

www.tamararoseblodgett.com

Made in the USA
Monee, IL
20 June 2020